BORN HEARTLESS II

T.J. Edwards

Lock Down Publications and
Ca$h
Presents
BORN HEARTLESS II
A Novel by *T.J. Edwards*

Born Heartless 2

Lock Down Publications
P.O. Box 870494
Mesquite, Tx 75187

Copyright 2019 T.J. Edwards
Born Heartless II

Lock Down Publications
Like our page on Facebook: Lock Down Publications @
www.facebook.com/lockdownpublications.ldp
Cover design and layout by: **Dynasty Cover Me**
Book interior design by: **Shawn Walker**
Edited by: **Sunny Giovanni**

T.J. Edwards

Stay Connected with Us!

Text **LOCKDOWN** to 22828 to stay up-to-date with new releases, sneak peaks, contests and more…

Thank you!

Submission Guideline.

Submit the first three chapters of your completed manuscript to ldpsubmissions@gmail.com, subject line: Your book's title. The manuscript must be in a .doc file and sent as an attachment. Document should be in Times New Roman, double spaced and in size 12 font. Also, provide your synopsis and full contact information. If sending multiple submissions, they must each be in a separate email.

Have a story but no way to send it electronically? You can still submit to LDP/Ca$h Presents. Send in the first three chapters, written or typed, of your completed manuscript to:

LDP: Submissions Dept
P.O. Box 870494
Mesquite, Tx 75187

DO NOT send original manuscript. Must be a duplicate.

Provide your synopsis and a cover letter containing your full contact information.

Thanks for considering LDP and Ca$h Presents.

T.J. Edwards

Chapter 1

I spent that whole night breaking down inside Miss Jackie's bathroom. We got the call that my mother had passed on two hours after we'd left her hospital room. A part of me felt like that she'd held on for as long as she did because she was waiting to see me for the last time. At least that thought gave my heart just a tad bit of peace. My mother was my everything. My heart and soul. There was nothing that I would not have done for her. Her whole life, all she'd known was pain and torment. Cursed, and born to parents that never loved, nor cared about her. Then cursed again to fall into love with a man that would be ten times worse than them. She'd been poor her entire life and had never seen outside of the slums of Chicago. As I kneeled over the toilet, purging my guts, all of these thoughts played through my mind, torturing me.

Sodi knocked on the door about an hour after I'd finished throwing up. "Papi, let me in. I need to be in there comforting you. You matter to me. Please let me be there." She begged.

By this time, I was so sick and weak that I needed somebody to hug on to. Somebody that cared about me. Somebody that understood what I was feeling in that moment. I needed to be loved. I was at my lowest point and falling fast. So, I opened the door.

She came in and fell to her knees, wrapping her arms around me. "I'm so sorry, Papi. I know you must be dying inside, but just know that I am here and that I ain't going nowhere. I love you with all of me. I mean that." She laid her head on my big chest. Started crying herself. For me this was big.

I didn't understand how a female could feel for me the way she appeared to be feeling for me. I didn't know what to think or what to do, so I just continued to break down with her in my arms until I couldn't cry no more.

Jelissa came to the bathroom door and knocked on it. "TJ, I got your sister on the phone. She's begging to talk to you."

I was so weak that I didn't even feel like talking to her. "Tell her I'll call her back in a few minutes. My head too fucked up right now." I felt sick again, like I needed to puke.

Sodi eased back and looked me over. "Baby, are you kidding? That's your sister. Your mother just told you to protect her. Get your ass up and go and get that phone. Now." She hopped up and pulled me along with her.

I lowered my head. "I can't think straight, Sodi. I gotta go identify my mother's body. Man, she was only thirty-four years old. This shit ain't fair." More tears dropped from my eyes. My knees got weak.

Sodi took a deep breath and held my face in both her hands. She had a habit of doing this. "Papi, listen to me. It sucks that Deborah is gone. It really does. We're going to go and identify her body together. We're going to give her a funeral together. And we're going to bury her together. But, baby, the bottom line is that she's gone. She's no longer here. Marie is. Your mother told you specifically to save her. That was her dying wish. You have to do this for her."

More knocking on the door. "She says she really needs to talk to you, TJ. That it's a matter of life and death."

Sodi looked into my eyes. "Save that girl, TJ. You have to do this for your mother." She opened the door and handed me the phone. "Here, Papi. I'm here with you."

Man, I was glad that she was because my brain was all screwed up in the worst way. I needed her guidance. She was like an angel sent from heaven. I was falling for her hard. I took the phone and placed it to my ear. "You know our mother is dead, don't you?" A lone tear slid down my cheek. Sodi wiped it away.

Marie was quiet for a brief second. "No, I didn't know that. When did she pass?" Her voice was scratchy. Almost as if it was filled with sleep.

"A few hours ago. I'm about to go down there and identify the body. You should come, too. I miss you, lil' sis."

She was real quiet. But then I could hear her sniffling away from the phone. She appeared to be crying. "I'm pregnant, TJ, and Deion says that he's going to kick this baby out of me. Daddy knows about it, and he says that the next time he sees me, he's going to shoot me down where I stand. I'm so scared that I don't know what to do. I feel trapped. You have to come and get me before something serious happens. I don't know what to do and I'm freaking out big time. I think when he gets back that he's going to do something to me."

I perked up and got angry quick. "Who? Who finna do something to you?" My heart was pounding in my chest.

"Deion. I think he's going to kill me, TJ, and I'm not kidding. I heard Daddy telling him that he needed to get rid of me. I don't know what that means, but I can only imagine. You know how our family gets down. Especially them. Deion doesn't want it to get out that he may have me pregnant. And Daddy is jealous, and crazy. He's been wanting to do something to me for a long time, but Deion hasn't let him. Now I think they are going to kill me and get rid of my body like they did Kia's."

I didn't know who Kia was, but it was blowing my mind that this conversation was actually happening. How the fuck could all of the men in my family be corrupting my little sister like this to the point that they were about to kill her out of jealousy of one another, and stupidity? I was thrown. "Sis, where are you right now?"

"I'm at Deion's place in Riverdale. He took all of my clothes and shoes and locked me in this room from the outside. The windows have bars on them, and outside of the bars are boards. I can't even tell if it's night or day. The only way I was able to call you is because when he let me out to use the bathroom, he was on the phone in the kitchen and I smuggled my phone back into the room before he locked the door again. What do I do? Should I call the cops?" She whimpered.

I was so lost and mad that I couldn't think straight. I was seeing red. My heart was banging against my ribcage. "N'all, fuck the law. I'ma be over there as soon as I get done identifying mama's body. I should be your way in like two hours. Do you think you can hold up until then?"

There was a loud slam in her background. She yelped. "Who is there?" She hollered.

I couldn't hear their response. "Who did they say, lil' sis?" I made my way into the guest room, getting dressed with one hand.

"Baby what's the matter? Is she okay?" Sodi asked, rubbing my back.

I held up a finger to silence her. She nodded in understanding and sat on the bed beside Jelissa who was rocking her son to sleep. "Marie, who is it?" I was getting worried.

"JD and Daddy. They unlocking the locks on this bedroom. I think they finna do something to me, TJ. Please get here soon." She cried. "Y'all leave me alone until Deion get back!"

I heard a bunch of commotion in the background.

"Come here, bitch! It's my turn now. Then Pops's. Then we gon' dump yo' ass in the river. Ma'fuckas done with you!" JD hollered, and Marie screamed.

"Bitch ass nigga, leave my sister alone!" I snapped.

This made Rae'Jon wake up crying at the top of his lungs. Jelissa scooped him and ran out of the room, apologizing.

I grabbed a .40 Glock out of the top dresser drawer and slid it into the small of my back. "Yo, I gotta go get my sister. She think my brother and father about to do something serious to her. And she pregnant right now. Everything is fucked up."

Sodi's eyes got as big as saucers. "Baby, I'm sorry. Is there anything I can do to help you?" She asked, throwing her spring jacket on.

"Just stay here and make sure that Jelissa and her son are okay. I'ma send Juelz a quick text and have him meet me in the Hunnits. Baby, I'm finna get rid of these niggas once and for all. Then I'ma go and identify my mother's body."

Sodi blocked my way as I was headed out of the bedroom. "Papi, wait. Can I please go with you? I feel like something major is about to happen, and I just want to be by your side. Please don't deny me of this." Her voice was shaky. I could tell that she was on the verge of breaking down. She was very emotional, and honestly it was one of the things that I loved about her. I needed that because at times I was so heartless that I needed to be balanced out. She kept me grounded.

"Baby, I need you to be here where you are safe and sound. I don't know what is about to transpire. But whatever it is, I'm gon' survive it, and when I do, I need to know that you're going to be waiting for me on the other end. You hear me?" I snatched her up and kissed her juicy lips. Seeking strength from them and got some. I honestly was starting to see just how much she was needed in my life.

She hugged me tight. "Baby, please be safe. Please don't lose this war, or whatever it is. I need you. You're my Papi now."

I kissed her forehead. "I won't, baby. But I gotta do what I gotta do. Just pray for me."

* * *

Juelz pulled behind Miss Jackie's truck a half hour later. Jumped out of his whip with a long black trench coat on and knocked on the passenger's window hard. I popped the lock, and he climbed in and showed me the assault rifle that he'd hidden in his coat. "Bruh, I'm telling you now that I'm shooting to kill. I hate your brothers. Them niggas real foul, and now that I know what they been doing to Marie, all I can think about is murder. When we get over here, I'm looking to kill, TJ. Fuck everything else. No nuts, no glory. That's my word. I'ma ask you one time, are you all in like a Poker hand?"

I nodded. "Hell yeah. But we gotta hold fast until we get Marie out of their care. As soon as she's out of danger, then we can let these bullets fly. Fuck them niggas. On everything." I pulled away from the curb and through the streetlights. It was four in the morning and beginning to rain. "How many shots that bitch hold?" I asked looking to him.

"Fifty. But I got two magazines in my pocket. I wanna make these niggas my Cover Girls. Word up."

I snickered at that and frowned. "My moms passed away a few hours ago. She said she couldn't take it no more and gave up her fight to Jehovah. I'm fucked up, bruh. I feel like I'm losing my mind." The rain began to come down a bit harder. I flipped on the windshield wipers and added some heat.

"Yo, I'm sorry to hear that, bruh. She was a good woman. A queen. It sucks that she had your old man as a husband. Anybody could see that he didn't deserve her."

"I know. He beat her senseless while she was on her deathbed. What type of nigga a get down like that on the mother of his children? I should've smoked that fool when I had the chance before he took the stand on me. Something told me to smoke him, too. Had I did it, my mother would still be alive." I shook my head. "What you got to smoke on?"

He took a fat ass Garcia Vega from his inside trench coat pocket. "Here, this that Brooklyn right here." He flicked his lighter and held it to the tip of the blunt while I puffed on it. "This shit gon' fuck you up, so take it easy. I don't want you being off of your square and shooting innocent bystanders and shit. A few pulls should be good for you."

I slowed the truck so I could stop at the red lights. Once I stopped, I let him hold the flame to the end, and I started to toke on it to get the cigar lit. Smoke wafted toward the roof of the truck. The weed smelled stanky and started cutting into my throat right away. I closed my eyes and started to cough. I heard the screeching of brakes. That made me open my eyes back up.

Juelz jumped closer to the passenger's door and struggled to get the big assault rifle up. "Aw, shit! It's a hit, TJ! It's a hit!"

The next thing I knew, there was a bunch of gunfire, and the windows shattered inside the truck. Hot liquid sprayed across my face, and I felt the burning sensation of lead entering into my body back to back.

Chapter 2

Boom! Boom! Boom! Boom! Two more shots seared into my back before I was able to step on the gas and storm through the red lights breathing hard. My throat was dry. I could taste blood. My shirt stuck to me. I could feel blood oozing down my back and into my pants. My vision became blurry.

"Drive this ma'fucka, TJ. I'm hit! I'm hit, bruh! Fuck!" Juelz hollered. He leaned on his passenger's door and pointed the assault rifle toward the back window as I drove away. He fired rapidly, and climbed into the backseat, spraying.

My vision seemed to be getting worst. I flew past the traffic lights and into a busy intersection. Swerved to miss an oncoming gray car and wound up driving over a boulevard. The truck kicked up grass. I kept my foot on the gas. The whip bounced before slamming back onto the street. Sparks flew from under it. Our enemies were in hot pursuit. A black van sped up to get beside our truck. The side door of the van was wide open. Two masked gunmen sat on the floor with Techs in their hands. Blue bandanas covered the lower portions of their faces. Fire spat from their fully automatics.

Boom! Boom! Boom! Boom! The side windows blew out. The glass popped all over the truck causing me to swerve like crazy.

"Fuck you waiting on, Juelz? Blow back at them niggas, bruh! Hurry up!" I looked into my rearview mirror and saw Juelz climbing off of the floor. His shirt was matted to him as well. It was caked with blood.

He positioned his assault rifle on the back window and got to shooting. His spent shells popped upward hitting the roof of the car, before landing on the floor by his feet. He kept right on shooting. The van swerved and slammed on its brakes. Its front windshield cracked up. Then Juelz put eight big holes inside of it before it shattered.

The shooters from the side van door jumped out of it and began firing at us as I did the best I could to drive away from the scene. Juelz kept popping until his rifle clicked and ran empty.

He laid on the floor and pulled the old clip out, sliding a new one into it. "This bitch hot, TJ. I can smell the metal burning, and it's damn near too hot for me to hold. You betta step on that gas."

I did. But as my foot stepped on the pedal, my eyesight became so blurry that I could barely see. I closed them for a second. Heard a car blow its horn at me. This made me open them as wide as I could. I veered back into the right lane. My shirt was soaked in my own blood. I was struggling to maintain my consciousnesses. I turned onto Ashland. "Juelz, I gotta pull over. I'm fucked up, bruh. I'm finna pass out."

"What?" He made his way back to the passenger's seat. "Nigga, what's the matter? Aw, shit!" He raised the assault rifle again.

Before he could blow at the niggas that had just rolled beside me, a masked shooter sitting on the edge of the passenger's side window got to bucking at our truck with a shotgun. *Bloom! Bloom! Bloom!* His bullets smacked the truck so hard that it rocked.

Another car appeared behind us. They got to airing at us. This was life in Chicago as we knew it. When niggas went to war here it was best that you knew that your enemies were going to go all out. The city was full of cutthroat, low life savages that fed off of guns and murder at all cost. In this city, a nigga would kill you, and an hour later be laid up with your sister like that shit never happened.

"Lean yo' head back, nigga!" Juelz ordered, aiming out of my window.

I did. "Slay them niggas, bruh!"

He busted his rifle. I could hear and feel the bullets flying past my face. Zipping by one after the other. The scent of burned gunpowder lit up the truck. My ears were ringing worst and worst each time he busted. I felt like I was going deaf in my right ear. I made a strong right on to Halstead and wound up nearly tipping the truck over. Juelz fell to the floor. I jumped on the Expressway and stomped the gas pedal to the floor. My eyes were bucked wide open. They kept trying cross. I was feeling woozy and drunk.

Juelz held his hand over his right shoulder. "They got me like four times, bruh. These bitches hurting, too." He gritted and fell against the leather seat of the truck.

I could feel my own bullet injuries. I had been shot in the back twice for sure. My right arm was also going numb. Blood dripped off of my fingers. The tips of them were tingling worse than I ever remembered. "I'm fucked up too, bruh. I gotta get to Marie though. They gon' kill my sister. I know they is." I jumped off of the Expressway and flew into Evanston.

By the time I made it onto Miss Jackie's block I was so woozy that I could no longer see or control my foot. I stepped on the gas. My eyelids closed. I felt the car hop

17

the curb. It rolled for a second and then crashed into a fence full of barking dogs. My face landed on the steering wheel and stayed there. The horn blared and I couldn't do nothing to stop it.

**

When my eyes opened again, Sodi and Jelissa were pulling me from the truck and loading me into Miss Jackie's G Wagon. They laid me flat on my back. Somehow someone had already put plastic down. Juelz sat in the passenger's seat. Sodi kneeled beside me. Jelissa jumped behind the wheel and started the Wagon.

Sodi rubbed the side of my face. "Papi, please fight. Please. I swear to God I need you. I need you so, so bad." She whispered.

"What happened to y'all? Did Deion do this?" Jelissa hollered.

I couldn't answer her. All I wanted to do was close my eyes. The pain was killing me. I felt like I was lying in a puddle of blood. The bullets felt like burning coals inside of me. On top of that I was struggling to breathe. I didn't know if it had been my brother that hit us up, or any of the other many enemies that me and Juelz accrued over the years. We were in the streets. Juelz more than me, but in Chicago that didn't matter. Enemies came for more than bloodshed here. Enemies came to send yo' ass to the reaper at all cost. It was all a part of the game. A Game that me and my right-hand man were knee-deep in.

My eyes attempted to roll into the back of my head. My lids closed. As soon as I felt comfortable enough to doze off, Sodi smacked me hard on the right cheek jolting me awake. "Stay ya' ass up, Papi. Fight that shit. Come on now, nigga. I need you. Jelissa, I need you to push this Wagon, girl. Get my nigga to the hospital like ASAP."

"Hell n'all. They gon' lock us up." Juelz mumbled.

"What?" Sodi asked, smacking me lightly on the cheek.

Juelz growled. "Arrgh, fuck." He turned around so he could face us. "In Chicago, if a ma'fucka come in with gunshot wounds, they gon' lock they ass up. Especially if you got records like me and bro got. You need to drive us across the border. Indiana don't be on that fuck shit. Even if they try it, all we gotta say is that we were robbed coming out of one of their clubs in Gary."

"Gary? TJ ain't finna make it that long!" Sodi snapped. "Drop us off at the nearest hospital now, Jelissa. I swear to God if my nigga die, I'm killing both of y'all asses. Now drop us off!"

"Girl, I got you. Calm ya' ass down. Word up." Jelissa said in her New Jersey twang.

"Yo, I don't give a fuck where y'all finna take bruh, I ain't going. I already know what they finna do to him after they finish healing his ass. They finna lock his ass right up. This ain't my first time getting hit up. Bruh, you need to listen to me. If you ain't trying to be back in the bing, you need to hold out until we get to Indiana. Them ma'fuckas out there don't be caring about this type of shit that Chicago do."

My eyes kept rolling into the back of my head. I felt like a wet sponge that somebody was stepping on. I was also freezing. I started shivering so bad that Sodi wrapped me into her arms. "Take me to Indiana. I ain't going back to jail. Fuck them people. I can't do that shit no more."

"Papi, no. You are losing a lot of blood. We can't risk trying to take you all the way to Gary. If we don't make it in time I could lose you. I'm not trying to do that again. You're going to the hospital here in Chicago. We have to roll the dice." Sodi said, resting her lips against my forehead.

"That's where I'm taking him anyway. I'll drop Juelz off after we get him straight. He don't look like he bleeding as bad as TJ is." Jelissa explained.

Juelz groaned, and shivered. "I don't give a fuck if I was. I ain't going back to jail. I'd rather bleed out than go back to that muthafucka."

Jelissa pulled the G Wagon into the Chicago Medical Hospital Parking lot. She threw it in park and rushed around to pull my door open. "Come on, Sodi, let me help you with him."

Sodi slowly slid from beside me. She wrapped her arm around my waist and eased me out of the truck. "Come on, Papi. I got you. We gon' get you into this hospital and get you all taken care of. Please keep fighting."

I was drenched in blood. My whole body felt like it hurt. Each step that I took seemed like it was going to be my last. My head was spinning like a twister. I felt nauseous, and as if my body was trying to turn itself inside out.

"Yo', Jelissa, let her take him inside! Come get me the fuck up out of here before Twelve be breathing down our necks!" Juelz hollered.

"Nigga, hold ya' horses. We gotta make sure TJ straight! Then, I'ma roll ya' ass to Gary. You bet not die on me neither!" She hollered.

Even though I was fucked up I couldn't help laughing at that. Only for a split second though. They got me into the lobby of the hospital, and my knees gave out. I collapsed right there on the floor. I just couldn't hold my own weight any further.

"Aw shit! Help! Help! We need a doctor. He's been shot multiple times. Help us!" Sodi screamed.

I lay on my back looking up at the ceiling of the lobby. I couldn't hear. Everything started to go blurry. A bunch of nurses rushed to my side. Things went black. When I opened my eyes again, I was being hoisted onto a hospital gurney. Then I passed out again. I could hear the beats of my heart pounding in my chest. Then there was a low-pitched hum. My eyes shot open. A white nurse placed an oxygen mask over my face. There was a pinch on the back of my hand. They zipped me down the hallway at full speed. Sodi ran beside the gurney with tears streaming down her perfect face. Two male doctors stopped her. The gurney kept on going. My eyelids became too heavy. I closed them. Everything faded to black.

***

"You betta fight, Jahrome. You gon' let them lil' boys kill you like this? Huh? Who gon' take care of Marie? Who gon' save her? I can't believe you letting this happen," came my mother's voice.

I stirred and sat up. The white sheet fell off of me. It was wet with my blood. I looked down and saw that I was sitting on a slab in the morgue. It felt cool under me. There was a tag on my toe. The room smelled of ammonia and embalming fluid. I looked around the morgue to see my mother standing under the bright lights that were directly above the door. Her long, curly hair fell to her sides. She wore a white robe like those in the choir at our church. Her hair covered her face. She was barefoot.

"Mama, what's going on? Why are you here?" I tried to get off of the slab, but it was impossible. It felt like I was pinned there.

She took a step forward. Pointed at me. "I'm disappointed in you."

"Why, mama? I tried to get there. I swear to God I did. But they shot me up. Them niggas caught me slipping."

"It's your fault, Jahrome. Your sister is dead. Marie died. They killed her. Your sick ass father. He did it. He did it and it's all your fault!" She snapped. She moved her hair out of the way, and I was able to see that she didn't have a face. It was blank. Almost as if God forgot to fill it in. She stood in front of me. "First me, now Marie. I knew I couldn't trust you. I hate you, TJ. You hear me? I hate you!" She raised her hand to slap my face.

Before she could, Marie appeared. She grabbed her hand and held it. "It's not his fault, Mama. TJ loved me. It was just my time. I was ready to go. I'm in a better place." She smiled. "I love you, TJ. I'll never forget you." She stepped closer to the bed to kiss my cheek.

Deion appeared. He grabbed her by the throat and flung her to the ground. Laughing at the top of his lungs. "When I say die, bitch, you die. Ain't nobody finna find out what you got inside of you." He raised a knife over his head and brought it down at blazing speed. "Ahhhhh!"

They all disappeared. The two Spanish cats from the bar that I'd slain arose from the ground. They walked over to the slab with blood dripping from the bullet wounds that I'd given them. Both dragged their feet like zombies. They spoke in unison. "Why. Did. You. Kill. Us. TJ?

Your soul will rot in hell. Why. Did. You. Kill. Us. TJ? You belong to him now."

Over their shoulders I could see the Devil. He appeared in a ball of fire. His eyes the color of electricity. He opened his mouth to reveal razor sharp teeth. "You belong to me now, TJ. Rest. In hell!" He hissed.

The two victims from the bar held out their arms for me. Their faces began to melt. "TJ. TJ. TJ. TJ." They chanted as one voice.

I struggled to break free. I was bound. The heat from the devil began to sear me. I shook as hard as I could. "Ahhhh!"

T.J. Edwards

Chapter 3
Eight Months Later

Sodi stood by the gates to the Cook County Jail jumping. Her long hair blew in the wind like crazy. I couldn't help smiling as I balanced my bag and made my way to the gates were she awaited me. It was mid-April. The sun shined bright in the sky with the exception of clouds that would block its rays every so often. The clouds were dark. They looked as if they were set to gather together so they could produce a sufficient amount of rain. Even if they did I wasn't about to let the weather rain down on my parade. I had just been released from the Cook County Jail after serving eight months. Eight months that my probation officer had revoked after finding out that I had been a part of a major shootout in the city of Chicago. I still hadn't gotten wind of who'd put the police in my business. But I intended on finding out soon enough. For now, my sole focus was on getting some Puerto Rican pussy and celebrating my nineteenth birthday in a week.

I stepped in front of the big gate and watched it move to my right. It screeched and clicked. It seemed like it was taking an eternity to open. Me and Sodi locked eyes the entire time. I could already smell her perfume. Her Fendi dress flapped in the wind. She had her long, curly hair down. It looked like it fell just below her waist. I couldn't wait to wax that ass.

As soon as the gate moved all the way to the side, she rushed me, and jumped in the air, wrapping her thighs around my body. I held her up. Our lips touched, and then we were kissing hungrily. I couldn't help gripping that ass.

"I missed you, Papi. Mmm." More kissing. "I swear I missed you so much. I thought you would never get home." Her tongue slipped into my mouth.

I crashed into the gate with her after it closed. I was already breathing hard. Piece rocked up ready for action. My teeth attacked her neck. I sucked. "Damn. Boo, you got me ready to take yo' lil' ass down right now." I sucked some more.

There were four other females there at the gate waiting for their loved ones to be released. They never took their eyes off of us as far as I could tell. Two of them looked just as bad as Sodi. I tried not to focus on that. Especially since she held me down for eight months straight. She hadn't missed a visit unless we agreed on it. And the only time we agreed it was cool for her to miss one of those was so she could attend her college classes at the university.

She got down and mugged the other females, then grabbed my hand. "Come on, baby. Let's get up out of here. I got some real freaky thangs I wanna do to yo' lil' sexy ass." She purred and winked at me.

I watched her ass jiggle all the way to her platinum Lexus truck. The dress kept on getting wedged into her ass cheeks. It looked real good to me. She still appeared to be small up top, but down low she was strapped. Thicker than I remembered. Visiting her through the glass for eight months straight had done little to help me to understand just how strapped she really was. She popped the back of the truck so I could place my bag inside of it. I did and followed her back to the front of her whip. "Yo, who the fuck copped this for you?" I asked, giving the truck a onceover.

She smiled. "Aw, so you see a bad bitch with a nice whip and you automatically thinking that some nigga had to give it to me, is that it?"

I stepped up to her and into her lil' pretty ass face. "Answer my ma'fuckin' question. Who the fuck copped this whip for you?"

She stared into my eyes for a short moment. Cars rolled past behind us. Some of them pulled into the lot. I guessed they were there to pick up somebody they loved who was getting out of jail just like I had. "TJ, you just getting out. I been holding you down the entire time. Nigga, you owe me some love and affection before we get to arguing and shit." She rolled her eyes and got into the driver's seat, slamming her door.

I walked around. The passenger's door popped open. I got inside. "Yo, you ain't gotta tell me shit, it's good. Let's just roll so I can give you what you want." My nostrils flared. I was irritated.

Sodi was just eighteen like me. She had just turned eighteen in February. I knew she'd just got a lil' gig working at a nail salon, but I knew that she wasn't checking a bag like that already. Some nigga had to be hitting her hand. It was the only thing that made sense to me. She pulled away from the curb. "My brother bought me this truck for my birthday. He knee-deep in the game now. So deep that he even got Juelz busting moves for him. But of course, you gon' find all of that out when you bump heads with ya' boy. I just hope it's more sooner than later because I been missing you like crazy, and I really wanna spend some time with you." She looked over at me. A few raindrops hit her windshield.

"How you know I'm finna fuck with, bruh? That nigga only came and seen me one time while I was in there. That ain't how shit supposed to have went down."

"I'm surprised he came and seen you at all. Juelz been on some hot shit out here. He been bagging niggas for the right price. Warring with a bunch a niggas over East. He got that drip now, but still shit looking real grim for him. But once again, whenever y'all get up with each other you gone see." She sighed. "You heard about your sister right?"

I nodded. "Yeah, I still ain't in a place to talk about it. But I did hear. Ain't nobody speaking up about who actually killed her though?"

Sodi shook her head. "Nope." She kept driving. "It's just a bunch of fingers being pointed in every direction. You know how that shit go."

I nodded. "Yeah, I do."

"Your brothers out here eating now though. Word throughout the city is that they plugged in with some Arab dudes out of Phoenix. Deion supposed to be preaching in some temple, but as soon as the service is over he back in the streets. Hustling, and popping pistols. He got a bunch of them Malik Boys running under him now. He think he invincible too."

I clenched my jaw. I could feel my temper getting hot. "What's good with JD and Kalvin's punk ass?" Kalvin was my sperm donor. JD and Deion were my brothers. Brothers that I had been warring with since the beginning of time it seemed.

"They run under Deion. Although he ain't calling himself Deion no more. He calling himself Kaliffa."

I frowned. "Kaliffa? Where the fuck he get that name from?"

She shrugged. "He's a Moor now. Whatever that is."

"Yeah, well, fuck all three of them niggas. They gon' pay for what happened to my sister. I know it was one of them. She was trying to tell me that before the phone went dead. All of the sudden they find her dumped in a garbage can after being chopped to pieces. That's some bullshit right there."

Sodi nodded. "Look, Papi. I know you gotta hit the ground running and get on your feet, and I ain't gon' try and hold you back from doing your thing. But all I ask is that you give me some time between doing whatever you finna do. Can you promise me that?"

"Fo show. I got you, boo." I eyed them thighs again.

"Thank you, Papi."

I still couldn't take my eyes away from her lap. "Sodi, what you got on under that Fendi sundress?"

She batted her eye lashes. "You'll find out soon enough."

I took my seatbelt from across my chest. "You know how to drive with just yo' left foot?"

She nodded. "Yeah, but why?"

"Because, I been gone eight long months. I wanna see what this pussy taste like. I'm feening."

"But, Papi, we finna be at the Sybaris in like forty-five minutes." She drove on to the freeway.

I dropped to my knees and yanked her sundress backward as best as I could get it. Her thick thighs popped out all shiny and perfumed. I shivered. Pulled her right thigh from the left one. Her naked pussy peeked out at me. It looked golden, and plump. I sniffed as hard as I could and smelled it.

"Papi, get yo' ass up. Come on now, behave. This pussy ain't going nowhere. Trust me."

I didn't give a fuck what she was talking about. My face was in her lap. I kissed her right on her bald cat. The lips slightly opened. My tongue traveled her groove before I sucked on each flap of her monkey.

"Mmm. Papi, please wait." She arched her back as two fingers slid deep into her center. Now I could smell her just a hint. She smelled fresh. Cat with a hint of perfume.

I opened her lips as wide as I could and sucked on her pearl. Flicking my tongue while two fingers ran in and out of her at full speed. I needed to swallow her juices. I craved them. Being away from pussy for so long made me crave it every second of every day.

Sodi moved her leg as far to the right as possible. Her pussy popped all the way out. It looked like an opened peach with its pink interiors. The sight drove me insane. "Mmm, Papi."

"Pull this ma'fucka over. I want some of this pussy right now. Fuck that Sybaris."

"But I already booked the room. It ain't no refunds. We can only get a credit for another time, and the Sybaris stayed booked. It's one of the best get-a-way hotels in the whole Midwest," she groaned.

I sucked my fingers into my mouth. Her taste was salty with a hint of sweetness to it. "Baby, pull this ma'fucka off the road real fast. I just gotta hit this pussy one time, then we can go on our merry way."

"You promise?" She asked, switching lanes so she could get in the right one.

"Yeah, I promise." Two fingers slid back inside of her. I got to working them in and out at full speed.

By the time she pulled into a Walmart parking lot, she had caused a puddle to form in the middle of her leather seat. We climbed into the back and let the seat all the way down. She laid on her back with her thighs wide open. My face was between them going to work. I felt like I wanted to taste every part of her anatomy down there.

"Papi! Papi! Awww! Mmm! Shit! Wait!" She screamed, humping up into my face. My lips clamped down on her button. That pushed her over the edge. She came, shivering.

Her juices dripped off of my chin. They ran down my neck and into my shirt. Sodi had always had a wet shot on her. It was one of things that drove me crazy about her. I got up and got between them thick thighs. She unzipped me and pulled my piece out. "You want this dick too, huh, Mami?"

"Yes, daddy. Please. Hurry up." She groaned.

My pants fell to my ankles. I leaned forward over her and lined him up. She held her lips open. I sunk into her furnace and trembled; sinking to her depths. Her cat was as tight as a fist and as hot as a toaster. I couldn't play with it. I was too excited to be back between them thighs. I got to smashing that pussy at full speed. Long-stroking her like my life depended on it.

"Daddy. Daddy. Aw, Papi. Ooo. Shit!" Her nails dug into my shoulder blades. Her ankles wrapped around my lower waist. I could feel her hot breath on my neck. It smelled like Spearmint.

"Unn. Unn. Unn. Unn. Sodi. Baby. Damn, boo." I groaned, fucking her harder and harder. The Lexus truck rocked. The windows were already fogged up. It smelled like sex already. The scent was enticing.

She arched her back and screamed again. "Awww, fuck! I'm cumming!" Her cat got to squeezing me like a fist over and over again.

I plunged and yanked her to me. Kept pounding harder and harder remembering all of the pictures that she'd sent to me while I was on lock. I used to imagine what it was gon' be like when I finally got that pussy again. Now I was in it, and it was even better than I imagined it to have been. She rose all the way up and bit into my neck. I came back to back in her womb. Stroking deeper, and faster. Jerking like crazy. Laid on top of her for a second, then pulled out. My piece was still jumping like crazy. "Gimme this shit from the back now, Mami."

"Noooo. Come on, Papi. You promised me." She rubbed her cat and tried to close her pussy lips back. Her flower was wide open, oozing. That only made me wanna hit that shit some more.

"Aiight. Fuck it. But step on that gas. I want some more of this shit." I rubbed her box and slid two fingers back into her. She moaned and got up.

***

Five minutes later we were back on the road. She cruised as the sun began to set. "What are your plans, baby? You know where you gon' be staying yet? I hope not back with that old bitch Miss Jackie."

I shrugged. "I ain't even thought that far into things. Juelz told me to hit him up when I got out and he was gon' have a lil' spot for me. I guess that's what I'ma do."

She mugged me. "Nigga, stop playin' with me. You know damn well that you finna come and stay with me until you get on yo' feet. Fucking around with Juelz ain't gon' get you nothing but killed. That I know for sure."

"If you already knew I was finna come and stay with you until I got on my feet then why you playing these ma'fuckin' games? What you thought, I was finna grovel or something?"

"First of all, English is my second language. I ain't learn it until I was five years old. Secondly, I'm eighteen now and I still don't know what the fuck grovel mean. Lastly, if you know I got you then you should have just said that. Sometimes it's nice to hear that you know I'ma hold you down. Ain't that what I been doing ever since we been a part of each other?"

I nodded. "Yeah, it is." I had to admit that.

"Alright then, give me my props sometimes. That's all I ask."

I leaned over and kissed her on the cheek. "You got that, boo. I appreciate how you been going hard for me since day one. On some real shit, I do."

"You're welcome. Now, come on. You owe me a few lovey-dovey days before you hit the ground running with Juelz."

Chapter 4

Late that night, Sodi came out of the bathroom dressed in a red satin lingerie number. She even had the garter belt on, and the matching red see-through stockings. It complimented her golden skin complexion perfectly to me. Her long, curly hair fell past her waist. She'd done her make up just right. She stepped to the foot of the bed and placed her small hand on her hip. "You think you really ready to handle all of this?" She said this turning in a slow circle. I saw that the red thong sliced her plump ass cheeks down the middle. She was so strapped that I couldn't stop looking at her. My piece got to jumping over and over. I wanted to be back in her fine ass like ASAP.

I scooted down the bed. To the right of us a huge waterfall crashed into the pool. The room was dimly lit. There was a blue light inside of the pool that gave it a mystic effect. Ella Mae played through the speakers. Sodi's perfume slowly began to drift over to me. I stood in front of her and pulled her to me. "Shorty, you already know you looking good as hell right now. You want Papi to tear this lil' ass up?"

She looked up at me with her big, light brown eyes. "You think my assistant little?"

I gripped that ma'fucka, kneading it like dough. "N'all, boo, I ain't mean it like that. Bring yo' lil' sexy ass here." Our lips connected. I continued to rub all over her fat ass booty. Her heat was evident.

She moaned into my mouth and popped back on her legs. "Papi, I missed you so much. It was hard being out here for eight months without you, but I held you down like a true Queen. I swear on my mother I did." She turned her face sideways and slipped her tongue into my mouth.

I trapped it and sucked on it before sucking all over her juicy lips. My fingers slid into the leg holes of her thongs from the back. Her sex lips were already engorged. They opened like the petals on a rose. Her heat welcomed me into her lotus. Two fingers slid into her depths. While I sucked on her neck I worked them in and out. "You waited for me, Mami. Huh? You love a nigga like that?"

"Mmm." She threw her head back. "Yes, Daddy. Only for you. Now treat me like you supposed to." She gripped my piece and squeezed it.

I flipped her ass over and bent her over the king sized bed. One tug, and everything was off. I threw it to the floor and looked down at her box. The lips opened slightly. They glistened with her dew. I raised my hand a brought it down on that ass. *Smack!*

She jerked forward. "Uhhhh. Daddy. Mmm. Don't do that. Please." She groaned. But her breathing became labored. She looked over her shoulder at me. Moved her legs apart. Now her juicy cat was really visible to my sight.

"This how I'ma keep yo' ass in order. I'm Daddy, right?"

She nodded and sucked on her bottom lip. "Only you, TJ. Only you."

I kept rubbing all over those cheeks. "Aiight den. A ma'fucka finna have to jump knee-deep in this game. I'ma need a stomp down bitch on the side of me. The only ma'fucka I trust is you. You're my lil' Queen. But that don't mean that I ain't finna be getting all up in this ass when you fuck up. Do you understand me?" I squeezed her booty. I was getting excited. She had me hard as hell.

"Mmm. I understand. But you ain't finna be treating me like I ain't no boss bitch or something. Nigga, we equal."

Smack! Smack! Smack! Smack! My hand got to tearing that ass up. Her thick ass cheeks were jiggling and shaking like crazy. The turned a bright shade of red. I kept on at it.

"Mmm. Mmm. Papi. Mmm. Wait. Wait. Daddy!" She moaned. Her legs were spaced wide. Juices oozed out of her box and drooled down both sides of her thighs.

Smack! Smack! Smack! Smack!

She fell forward on her stomach. Kicked her knee up to her ribs. I sat beside her and got to fingering that pussy at full speed. Rubbing all over her ass. She gripped the bed sheets. "Daddy! Daddy! I'm cumming! I'm cumming! Aw, shit! I'm so sorry! I'm so sorry!" Then she was shivering like crazy.

I opened them cheeks and locked on to her clit. Sucking, and nipping at it lightly with my teeth. She really go to going crazy then. She screamed. I sucked like I was trying to pull her jewel out of her box.

I rubbed all over her ass and pulled her to the edge of the bed. Made her get up on all fours. Slid in and got to fucking her as hard as I could, watching my piece go in and out of her thick ass. Her big booty would open and close every time I plunged into her cat. A constant sound of swishing was loud coming from between us. I peeped at the way she received me. The lips to her pussy were dark and plump, dripping her essence. She felt hot, and real tight. I clutched them hips and really got to working her ass over. Groaning 'cause that shit was so good.

"Mmm. Mmm. Daddy. Yes. Yes. Mmm. Yes. Awww. Fuck me. Fuck me, Daddy. Yessssss!" She opened her mouth wide. Arched her back and came again. She fell on her stomach.

I kept pounding, obsessed with her intense heat, and now the smell of her fucked pussy. I grabbed her hair. "This Daddy shit, right? Tell me who this pussy belong to?" I growled fucking her harder and harder.

"Uhhhh! Yours, Papi! Yours, Daddy! Awww, please! Unn. Unn. Please, Daddy! It. It. Awwww-shit!" She started to shiver.

I felt her gap gripping me tighter and tighter and came. I couldn't hold back any longer. I fell on her back, pumping my seed into her.

She laid there biting the big pillow that was amongst a bunch more like it. Her ass tooted upward toward me. Her cat continuing to squeeze me over and over again.

I pulled out and stroked him, looking at her pussy from the back. Now it was a red shade of brown. The lips were crinkled. Something about the sight of it drove me crazy. I flipped her ass over and climbed on top of her. Pulled her up to the top of the big bed. The waterfall continued to surge into the big pool of the hotel beside us. The atmosphere was romantic, even though I had that killa shit on my brain. I wanted to beat that pussy in. Sodi was bad, and she had proven to be a good girl. I felt like I needed a good girl like her beside me. I didn't know where the streets were going to take me. But I knew that if I hit my lowest that she would be there to hold me down. She had already done it twice. So, I had to lock her ass down. In Chicago, one of the most important ways to lock down a woman was by fucking her brains out every time you got between those thighs. If yo' dick game was weak it wouldn't be long before the whole city found out, and then everybody got to judging your masculinity by your bedroom antics. I needed to lock her ass down, so I felt I had to do what I had to.

"Bring yo' lil' ass here, lil' baby." I yanked her to me and pushed those knees to her chest. Slid back into her box and popped both of her pretty titties out. The dark brown nipples erect, and juicy.

"Daddy, take it easy on me for a second. I want you to make love to me instead of just fuck. Aww. Aww. Aww."

No mercy on that pussy. I got to piping her down like it was finna be my last piece of cat. She dug her nails into my shoulders. Grabbed me down by the neck and sucked all over my face. It felt good. I felt like she was getting more and more freaky. I loved it. My hips sped up. My dick was like a battering ram. Harder and harder I plunged inside of her guts. It felt so good. The big bed shook while Ella Mae crooned out of the speakers.

"Daddy. Daddy. Cum in me. Uhhhh. Daddy. Wait."

More pounding. Harder, and faster. This bitch had to be crazy about me. I couldn't see it no other way. When you had a good woman in Chicago, one that would hold you down no matter the circumstances, you held on to her at any cost. Fuck what the so called players on the street said. I pulled her to me and hugged her while I fucked her with everything that I had.

She bit into my neck and screamed. I felt her walls gripping me, then she got so wet that I could barely feel anything down there. I came, shaking on top of her.

***

After our shower, we eased into the pool. I stood up against the wall while Sodi turned her back to my chest and rested her ass in my lap. We were both naked, and it felt so good to have a bad woman in front of me that was super thick. Her hair had curled up ridiculously. She was looking so sexy that I couldn't stop kissing all over her neck.

She backed up a lil' more. "TJ, would you think I'm crazy if I told you that I loved you?"

I licked all over the right side of her neck. My dick was already hard again. It poked between her cheeks, and nearly a quarter of it was lost from view. She backed up on me a lil' more, and winced. I could feel my head right on her rosebud. "N'all, boo, I wouldn't think you crazy. Why? You think you feeling me like that fa real?" I bit her neck kind of hard.

She shivered. "Daddy, I don't know. All I do know is that you drive me crazy. I wish we could just pack up and leave Chicago behind. I mean, I know we only eighteen and shit, but so what?" She turned around until she was facing me. Now my piece rested up against her stomach. "Would you leave with me if we could?"

I held her and looked into her light brown eyes. I was trying my best to not get mesmerized by her lil' ass. Having a bad bitch that you had conquered was one thing. But to have one that made you weak just from the sight of her was another. Sodi was so bad that I found myself stuck at times. On top of that, her pussy was so good. The best I'd had. But instead of going the soft route I knew I had to fuck with her mind a lil' bit. Bad bitches always expected niggas to fold just because of how they looked. Well I was out to change that narrative. "What make you think that

I'd just leave everything behind and dip off with you? I'm only eighteen. I got a whole ass life to live. A ma'fucka too young to be settling down and playing house."

She bucked her eyes, then lowered them. She looked hurt. "I wasn't saying it like that. I was just thinking that would avoid all of the drama here and just bounce. To be honest I'm a lil' worried about you. I don't know what these niggas in this city is getting ready to do to you."

"Fuck these niggas. I ain't finna run. My fate is already sealed anyway. You already know I believe in that pre-destination shit. I wrote you about that all the time."

"You also wrote me about leaving these streets alone. You said you wanted to be a writer. That you wanted to make your mother proud, and that you were gonna do right by me. What, you mean to tell me that all of that shit changed?"

I shook my head and gripped her ass. "N'all, but them niggas finna pay for what they did to my sister. They also gon' pay for hitting me up. Me and Juelz. Ain't no hoes over here, Sodi."

She placed my face within her hands. "I already know that, TJ. I know what type of man you are. But at the same time, how many chances do you think God is going to give you before he takes you off of this earth? Huh?"

I stayed silent. I didn't know the answer to that question. I didn't even know if I really cared either. I had so much hate in my heart that I knew the only thing that would settle it was murder. My mother and my sister Marie were my heart and soul. Both were gone. And the ma'fuckas that beat them into the ground and tortured them the most were still alive. Every second that they were I felt like they were shitting on both of my Queens' graves. I couldn't have that. I felt like I ain't have shit to live for. All I could see was murder and money. When it was my time to go I would be ready.

"Yo, I don't know what Jehovah got planned for me. When it happens though, it just happens. Can't nobody predict the future, and I ain't finna play pussy until then. Fuck that."

She sighed. Her fingers twisted one of my dreads. "I don't know what the future holds either, TJ. No matter what it does, I'll be here for you. I'll have your back until God takes us off of this earth. You need to know that. Also." She pushed me away from her and climbed out of the pool. Her juicy ass jiggled. She picked up a heavy terry cloth towel and proceeded to dry off with it. Then she went into the closet and pulled out a Gucci handbag. She took out a silver package and came back over to the pool. "Here, I know this ain't much but it's eighteen ounces of some eighty five percent China White. My brother say it's yours on GP. He say you can step on it twice and bring back a whole key. That when you ready to re-up to holler at him."

I smiled. "That's a half a thang?"

She nodded. "I really don't want you in those streets, but if that's the route you gon' choose, then let's do this shit to the fullest. I'm riding with you ten toes down. I love you, TJ, and nigga, I'ma make you love me back real soon, you gon' see. Now get yo' ass up and fuck me again from the back. See if you can earn more than that." She carried the half of a brick back to the bed and bent over it.

I almost broke my neck trying to get up out of that water. Yeah, I had to lock Sodi's ass down. There was no way around that.

Chapter 5

Juelz was cheesing like a Cheshire cat as I stepped out of the Sybaris two days later. He rested against his black and red Range Rover truck. He had that bad boy sitting on thirty-two-inch Parelli's. The paint shined in the sunlight. There was just a hint of a breeze. He started to walk up to me but stopped in his tracks as Sodi appeared out of the building. She stepped in front of me and pulled my head down so she could kiss my lips. I tongued her ass down for a full two minutes, rubbing all over that ass that she had encased in a Burberry skirt dress that clung to her every curve.

"Papi, remember, take care of what you gotta take care of. Then you meet me back at our place tonight. If anything changes, all I ask is that you call me and let me know. Don't be fucking off with them hoes out here either. Whatever you need from a bitch, you can get that shit from me. Do we understand each other?" She peered into my brown eyes.

I felt a twinge of weakness for her ass again, and knew I had to man up. "Shorty, you just gon' head and get shit situated. I'll get at you later, one way or the other. Aiight?"

She sighed. "Yeah, aiight then." She chirped her Lexus truck and opened the door.

Juelz threw his arms out. "Aw, what? You don't see a nigga or something? My mans done came home and now you ain't fucking with me?"

"Boy, I wasn't fuckin' with you when he was gone. Why would shit change all of the sudden?" She rolled her eyes.

"Aw, I see how shit go, Mamita. You done got all thick and shit, so you think you are the shit. Right. Cool. Keep stepping then. This finna be my city real soon. Then you and the rest of these hoes finna be kissing my ass."

Sodi smacked her lips. "Yo' mama a hoe, nigga. Betta watch yo' mouth, Juelz, fa real. Only man can turn me into a hoe is TJ." She rolled her eyes again and got into her truck.

Juelz mugged her, then waved her off. "Yo, let's get the fuck out of here, TJ. Yo' lil' bitch gon' fuck around and get her head busted. Straight up, shorty."

I laughed. I wasn't worried about him touching Sodi. That shit wasn't happening on my watch. I would never let things get that far. I eased into his Range Rover. The leather seats felt like I was sitting on a cloud. I adjusted it to my liking and slid the seatbelt across my chest.

Juelz was still talking to himself. I knew that Sodi had gotten under his skin. I could see that shit written all over his face. He clicked his seatbelt in place, after setting a Tech .9 on his lap.

"Nigga, where you get this truck from? This bitch stolen?" I wanted to know. Juelz was frivolous for hijacking ma'fuckas and rolling their hot ass whips for forty eight hours. I wasn't trying to get involved in nothing like that. The last place I wanted to be was prison.

"Ma'fuckas don't steal cars no more, nigga. Fuck wrong with you?" He snickered and turned up some Lil' Dirk. Got to bobbing his head.

"Nigga, a lil' less than a year ago you was out here robbing niggas for cars and shit. Don't act all brand new."

He laughed. "Ain't shit brand new about me other than this whip. This Tech and this muthafuckin' truck. This bitch was a gift. And so was this." He pulled out a thick knot of hundred dollar bills. All small faces. That threw me for a loop.

"Yo, who the fuck you rocking with that's paying you in small faces?"

He split the knot down the middle and handed me half. "That's ten thousand right there, bruh. It ain't much but you home now. We finna eat the way we supposed to. I got you."

I nodded. "That's what's up. Now answer my question."

He started the engine and pulled out of the lot with his shit knocking. It was bassing so hard that my ears kept popping. I turned it down. He mugged me. "Before I get into what I'm doing you need to know that as soon as Deion found out you were home, he put up a fifty-thousand-dollar bounty on yo' head. But you lucky though because it ain't to murder you. It's only for a person to bring you to him. Now what he gon' do to you once he get you is another story."

I frowned and got heated right away. "How the fuck he getting his hands on fifty thousand dollars to put on me?"

"That nigga up-up. He fucking with them Moe's over there on the eastside. He got two decks over there. Then he got a couple blocks in Moe Town too. I don't know how he pulled it off, but he running shit. They calling him a prince."

"A prince? Prince of what?"

"They whole lil' thang. They saying Jeff gave him that slot. That nigga got stupid power now." Juelz said, shaking his head.

I was in disbelief. My brother Deion was shysty. I couldn't see how anybody could run under his rotten ass. Everything he did had always been to benefit himself. I didn't know how he'd gotten the power he did but that spelled trouble for me. I had to take him out of the game as soon as I could, or shit was going to get real hectic real fast. The Moe's were a powerhouse within the city of Chicago. If Deion was calling for them I couldn't only imagine how deadly they had become.

"Ma'fuckas still don't know what exactly happened to Marie. It's a lot of speculations though. Supposedly they found her two days after we got hit up. Oh, and do you remember that nigga Blue?"

"Blue?" I shook my head. "That name ain't ringing a bell. Who the fuck is that?"

"You remember. Think back to when Punkin had her birthday party a lil' while back. That nigga Blue was the fool in the room that tried to take the pussy and you got off all up in his ass. Remember?"

"Aww. Yeah. What about that nigga?" I'd forgotten all about him.

"Well, word on the street is that it was him and his boys that hit us up. He a major nigga now too. He be in and out of Chicago though. Supposedly he moving some major weight up north in Wisconsin."

"Wisconsin? Ain't that full of white folks?" I asked, feeling like my head was spinning. Juelz was hitting me with a lot of heavy bombs all at once.

"N'all, it's plenty black ma'fuckas out there too. But anyway. He at your neck too. He ain't put no cheese up as far as I know, but he most definitely want ya' life according to his niggas that be pillow-talking with these hoes.

That shit been all over Facebook too. But you already know how shit goes. If them niggas want it with you they want it with me too. You my brother, and I'm down for whatever, bruh. Know that."

I didn't know what to think or to feel. I felt like I had the whole city out to get me. I couldn't even remember how Blue looked. That news coupled with the bullshit involving Deion was fucking my brain up. I didn't know what to do first.

"You gon' say something, nigga?" Juelz asked, lighting a blunt.

"Ain't shit I can say. I gotta get my cash up so I can be ready to perform when any of these niggas run up on me. This shit ain't sweet by no way. Ma'fuckas wanna take me out the game, then they gotta get this shit like animals." My chest got to heaving. I was feeling angry and murderous. "What's good with that Tech tight there?"

"This one?" He shrugged. "Shit, take it. It's yours. That bitch hold thirty. I'll get you some clips tomorrow." He kept rolling.

"Aiight, nigga, now tell me who you got this whip from?" I took the blunt from him and got to blowing that killa. The smoke was harsh. It tasted like how gasoline smelled.

"Remember the shit I was doing before you got locked up? You know the whole murder for hire thing?" He asked, pulling up to a stop light. The sun was really shining now. He had a cool water scented air freshener blowing through his vents. It smelled real good.

"Yeah, I remember."

"Well, nigga, I'm on that same shit. But the risk is higher. But so is the reward."

"Explain yo' self."

"I get fifteen bands for a body now. Well, fifteen for niggas, and twelve for bitches."

"What? So that's all you been on since I been locked down? Stanking shit?"

He nodded. "I done invested in this strip club that I run with that old bitch you used to fuck with. Miss Jackie. You remember her?"

I nodded. "Yeah, she dropped me a couple bands over the lil' eight months I was down. She a good girl. How the fuck y'all link up?"

"She like young niggas. She said I reminded her of you. She gave me the pussy, and then I wound up wearing that ass out on a few occasions. Once I made sure that she was dick-drunk, I moved in on her credit. Bitch financed the club and overseeing everything, even though I'm a fifty-one percent owner. You should start fucking back with her and get that lil' forty-nine percent up out of her so we can run this ma'fucka together. What you think?"

I was a lil' jealous. Juelz moved in on my vet bitch while I was away, and it was making me feel some type of way. I wanted to hit his ass in the jaw. "Bruh, what the fuck made you go in on my old bitch while I was locked away in the Bing?"

He shrugged. "Didn't think that bitch meant shit to you. If I did, I wouldn't have had my dick all in her mouth. Busting on her back and shit. But I did. Get over it. Like I said, you should see if you could get that forty-nine percent out of her. She ain't hurting for no cash. Her old man just got a two million-dollar lawsuit. That bitch rolling in the dough like a ma'fucka."

"Anyway, nigga, where you taking me right now?" I needed to switch the subject. I couldn't believe Miss Jackie had me feeling like a sucka because she had fucked my mans. I guess you couldn't stop a hoe from being a hoe no matter what you tried to do. But I was feeling sick a lil' bit. I was hoping I hadn't developed no feelings for her. But I wasn't sure. She held me down through a lot. And she had been my first real shot of pussy. Yeah, I think she had me.

"I wanna take you out North so you can meet one of my big homies. I know you trying to get your hands dirty so you can get yo' bands all the way up, so we on business on day one. I got a few moves lined up and I want you to be able to roll with me. That sound good to you?"

"I ain't got no fucking choice. I gotta eat."

***

His big homie threw me for a loop. First off, he was a big ass white boy with tattoos all over him. He stood about 5'10" and weighed two hundred plus pounds. Was bald and spoke low enough for you to miss every word if you didn't listen up. His name was Jay. We met up with him on the Northside of Chicago inside of a garage that had a bunch of high-priced Harleys and Crotch Rockets.

He and I shook hands. He stayed looking me in the eyes the entire time. Then we all sat around a round table. Jay had four members of his crew standing around in the shadows. Each man held a Doberman. The dogs looked lethal. They watched both me and Juelz's every move. I didn't know if they could sense the fear coming off of me, but they sure acted like it.

Jay grabbed a black duffel bag off of the floor and dug four stacks of money out of it. They were old faces just like the bills Juelz had given to me. "TJ, welcome home. I heard you been gon' for eight months. That's a long time to be away from the city of Chicago. Things tend to change pretty quickly. The only thing that didn't change while you were away was the need to stack that paper. In this city, if you ain't got no paper, you're nothing more than filth. You feel what I'm saying?"

I nodded. "So, how you finna help me out, white boy?" While in the county jail I'd been jumped twice and stabbed up by the Arians. They were a group of racist white boys that hated anything and anybody that wasn't like them. As I sat, staring at Jay, he reminded me of them.

He laughed. "Well, Black boy, I'ma help you by putting that cash in yo' pocket. Is there any other way?" He smiled and looked back at his homeboys.

"Say, homie, what's all this snickering and shit about? I don't see shit funny." I snapped ready to get off in his ass.

The Doberman were growling like crazy now. Jay mugged me. "Look, homie. I don't know who you are or what you got on yo' chest, but you need to let that shit off. We all about making money over here. If there is a problem though, we can definitely solve that shit." He snapped his fingers. Now the dogs were really growling. His men looked like they were having a hard time controlling them.

I stood up. "Fuck you saying then, white boy?"

Juelz jumped up. "Yo', chill, nigga. Damn. These white boys cool. I fuck with them the long way."

"What? Bruh, watch yo' mouth. Don't be calling me no nigga in front of these ma'fuckas." I was ready to go at his ass too.

Jay held up a hand. "Look, Juelz, get yo' boy on deck. I got this fifty gees. You know what it is. Handle this business that we discussed and it's yours. Simple as that. Calm him down though."

"Can't no ma'fucka calm me down but me." I saw a few of Jay's tattoos. I couldn't understand what they meant but I automatically equated them to something racist.

Juelz held up a hand and placed it around my neck. "Yo', Jay, we finna get up out of here. Something ain't right with my dude. But you can consider this one done." He grabbed the money off of the table and bowed his head. I could hear Jay laughing behind us as we made our way outside.

As soon as we got in the truck Juelz snapped. "Fuck wrong with you? Are you tryna to fuck off my plug?"

I shook my head. "Nigga, n'all. Let's just go and handle this business, I need half of that money so I can really get on my feet."

Juelz frowned. "Yo, nigga, I don't know what's going on with you but you better ice that bipolar shit like ASAP. If we finna be out here in this jungle together then you need to let me know what's going on inside of yo' head. Aiight?"

I nodded. "So we finna bust this shit down the middle or what?"

"You already know. Let's roll out."

T.J. Edwards

Chapter 6

"Aiight, so peep. I ain't gon' get into too much detail with everything, but peep. This nigga Jay fuck with them Cartel boys back out West and below the border. I'm talking Mexico. The Cartel ma'fuckas pay him to take care of anybody that might be a threat to their operations. Or ma'fuckas that's late on their debts. Now, the Cartel don't do that breaking bones and maiming shit. N'all. They don't get down like that. They take yo' ass out the game in the deadliest way possible. That's how they get down. I think they be liking they murders to be all crazy and shit, so it scare people from doing anything that crosses against them. Anyway, I met Jay back when we were in St. Charles a few summers back. He a good dude. His sister married to one of the main niggas that work under a Cartel boss. He plugged him into the removal side of the operations. And Jay plugged me in."

I looked at this nigga like he was stupid. We were sitting inside of a Trailer Park, outside of Rockford, Illinois. "Nigga, you saying all that shit to tell me what?"

Juelz exhaled loudly. "Bruh, we gon' handle the removal part of shit. It's like I told you before. Jay pay me fifteen bands for each dude I get rid of for him, and twelve for each female. His only ask is that when I take a ma'fucka out that I make that shit look good. His position inside of the Cartel is banking on every move that I put down. If I botch one, they gone get up with him. And he in turn is gone get up with me. I ain't trying to have a bunch of crazy ass white boys rolling around Chicago looking to fan my ass down. I already got enough of our people looking to do that." He looked out of the window and into the night. We were surrounded by rundown trailer homes.

"Aiight, that sound good. But what are we doing here?" I followed his gaze and looked around at all of the homes. They were gray, and dirty looking. I felt uncomfortable because I had never been in a trailer home before and I didn't know what to expect.

He nodded out the window. "You see that trailer home over there with the red blanket hanging on the railing?"

I looked around until I found what he was talking about. "Yeah, I see it."

"Well, we finna go in there and make sixty thousand dollars. He already paid me thirty up front."

I was already calculating the move. I figured if we were getting paid sixty gees that it meant we were slaying two dudes and one female. That would be sixty on the head. Unless we were smoking five broads. That didn't seem logical though. But then again, I didn't know fully what we were handling. All I knew was that I needed that thirty gees. "So, what's the move?"

"Two niggas, one bitch. They thinking we coming to cop some of that crystal shit from them. But you already know what it is." He pulled out a .9 millimeter and tightened the silencer inside of it. "You let me do all of the talking. Here. You just carry this bag right here. They gone think it's money. Before they get on to us I'ma finish they ass. All you gotta do is help me dice some shit up after I put 'em down. Aiight?"

"Fuck you mean dice?" I was confused. I needed to make sure that it wasn't some term that I wasn't familiar with.

"Chopping, nigga. After I handle this business we gone chop 'em up into itty bitty pieces. That word ain't got no other choice other than to get out. Soon as it does Jay gets his praise, and we get ours."

"Bruh, why it seem like you trying to please this white dude?" I asked, as he handed me a book bag.

"You just tripping because you don't understand what's going on right now, but you will when the time is right. For now, just follow my lead. Remember, I'm doing all of the talking." He opened the driver's door. The truck started to ding like crazy, indicating that the door was open.

I jumped out and walked beside him. Surveying the area, the whole time. I could hear more than a few trailers playing Rock and Roll loud as hell. I felt that would help us out in the long run. There was barely any grass. It smelled like motor oil and manure. I felt my Desert Eagle in the small of my back. It didn't have a silencer on it, and I didn't give a fuck. If I had to use it, it was with no mercy.

Juelz stepped up on the trailer steps and knocked on the door. The knocking sounded loud in the night. He looked down at me and then back to the door. He appeared tense. His face was expressionless. I could tell that he was allowing for his killa mode to come over him.

I looked both ways. Stepped closer to the bottom step. Listened to see if I could hear anything weird. The Rock and Roll from the other trailers were the only noise I could hear clear as day.

The door to the trailer opened. A tall, slim white dude with long, dirty blond hair poked his head out. He looked like Kid Rock. "What's up, man? Who you looking for?"

Juelz stepped closer. "My name Coogi. Jay sent me to cop some of that crystal shit that you got for sale. You are Sam, right?"

Sam gave him a suspicious look. "Long as I been fuckin' with Jay, he ain't never sent no Blacks over here. You sho he sent you?"

"Give him a call. Tell him that Coogi outside with the money right now. He'll let you know what's good."

Sam nodded. "Wait right here. I'll be back in a second." He stepped inside and closed the door back.

I was feeling anxious. I was wondering why we hadn't simply rushed inside, bucking whoever was on the other side down? All this slow shit seemed so uncomfortable. I didn't like it.

There was a full moon in the sky. Crickets chirped. It felt like it was every bit of eighty degrees. My forehead began to sweat. I felt nervous and out of bounds. I was ready to handle our business and get the hell out of there. I felt rusty and out of place. It seemed like Sam was taking a long ass time. I wondered if he was trying to set us up or something.

Finally, he opened the door with a Marlboro cigarette in his mouth. "Alright, come on in. He described the both of you to a tee. Let's take care of this little bit of business so the both of you can be on your way." He said with a deep voice.

Sam moved to the side and Juelz stepped into the trailer first. I walked in right behind him. The first thing I saw was a white female on the couch, bagging up with little Ziploc bags from a pile of Crystal Meth. Her face looked sunken in. She must have weighed less than a hundred pounds. She wore a white beater that was way too big for her. Through the arm holes I could see her ribs. She looked up from the dope and smiled. Her yellow teeth looked like they were caked with plaque. To the right of her was a heavy-set biker-looking man. He had on a dark leather jacket. His face was red. He wore a big, busy gray-ish-reddish beard. There were tattoos all over his face. He looked up at us and grunted. Then he went right back to doing his work.

Sam directed us into the small kitchen. He reeked of must and sweat. His hair was speckled with bits of dandruff. He wore a Newport shirt over cut off shorts, no socks, or shoes. The trailer was cluttered with all kinds of clothes and boxes. The table was a small, round one. There were dishes upon it with leftover foods and they had roaches crawling all over them. "So, since when have Jay stared fucking with the Blacks? He must be thirsty to take your dollars." Sam said, scratching his beard.

I sat down across from him. I didn't like him already. I also kept my eyes focused on the fat man and the female behind him. I saw that they were still bagging up their crystals.

Juelz sat down. He eyed Sam from across the table. "Jay taking our Black dollars ain't got nothing to do with you. Let's focus on the task at hand."

Sam smiled. He blew the cigarette smoke across the table into Juelz's face. "This ain't the ghetto, boy. You don't run shit over here. In my house, I talk about what I wanna talk about. And I question whatever I wanna question. You don't like it ,you can kiss my ass." He snapped.

Juelz sat there staring at him. "Is that right?"

"You got-damn right it is." Sam growled, leaning forward on the table.

I kept my eyes on the living room. The heavy-set biker kept on looking back toward the kitchen. I wondered if he was strapped. I didn't feel comfortable sitting down. I stood up and adjusted the bag on my shoulder. I kept my right hand free so I could get to the gun in the small of my back more easily.

"Why you standing, boy? You thank this is the fifties and you can't take a seat where you wanna sit?" He laughed.

Juelz frowned. "Jay say you're fifty thousand dollars behind on your front. You care to explain?"

Sam's eyes grew big. He lowered them and sat back. "Jay needs to keep my business to himself. Why the fuck would he tell some colored how much money I owe those Spicks that he work for? Far as I'm concerned, they can kiss my ass too. They won't get one smaller crumb from me. Now you can tell him that." He dug his index finger into his ear and shook it to scratch it.

Juelz laughed. "Yeah, how about I don't, and you say I did." He upped his pistol and pressed the barrel to Sam's left eye before pulling the trigger.

The left side of Sam's face tore off and landed on the floor of the trailer. Sam stood up hollering. He threw his hands in the air. His brains slowly dripped out of the missing portion of his face like spaghetti. Juelz stood up and placed his barrel to his forehead and pulled the trigger twice. Blowing the rest of his brains out of the back of his head. Sam crumbled to the floor.

The female stood up and got to screaming. "Oh my God! Oh my God! Sam! Sammy! No!"

The big biker reached on the side of the couch and came up with a double barrel shotgun. He slid two bullets inside of it and snapped it in place. Threw the woman to the floor and stepped over her. He stopped and aimed his gun directly at Juelz.

I dropped to one knee and lit his ass up. *Boom! Boom! Boom! Boom!*

He dropped the shotgun and flew backward. Four big holes decorated his chest and stomach. Blood oozed out of them like a pot overflowing.

The woman jumped up and looked for a place to hide. "Please. No. Don't do this. Sam was going to pay. He was going to pay; I swear!" She screamed.

Juelz rushed into the living room. He grabbed her by the neck and slammed his barrel to her forehead. He pulled the trigger twice and let her go. She slumped to the floor. The back of her head slowly oozed down the wall.

"Come on, bruh. Let's get the fuck out of here!" I hollered throwing open the trailer door.

Juelz was taking their dope. He threw it all into a pillowcase before rushing out into the night behind me. He opened the driver's door. Started the ignition, and stormed away after I jumped in. "That's how you do that shit, TJ. That's how you go in there and make shit happen, then get the fuck up out of there!" He exclaimed.

I nodded. My heart was beating fast as hell. I kept replaying the scenes in my head. I saw Sam's head getting blown off. Then the Biker filling up with holes. Then the woman getting her head blown off. I knew the images would stick with me for a lifetime. But I needed the money. And as much as I hated to admit it, I knew that I would be right back beside Juelz for his next job.

Chapter 7

A week later, and I had already pulled two other jobs with Juelz. I had a total of $40,000 to my name. I wanted to get about fifty before I got my own crib and copped me a lil' whip. In Chicago, $50,000 was chump change because the cost of living was so high. I knew that I had to get my money right first before I would be able to do anything else. From the way Juelz was talking, he was making it seem like Deion was loaded with cash, and an army. There was no way that I could go at his chin without having my money right. I needed weapons. I needed security. I needed my own place that I could lay my head.

A week after I got out, I was rolling around with Juelz when he pulled beside a raspberry droptop Jaguar. He rolled down my window. I looked over and saw that there was this bad ass caramel female inside of it. She had her hair permed all silky like. It was raspberry at the tips to match her car. Juelz blew his horn, and she looked over at us. Her face was familiar.

"Say, Punkin, guess who I got riding with me?" He asked, nodding at me.

Punkin's eyes got as big as saucers. "TJ! Fa real! Is that you?" She hollered. She threw her car in park and hopped out of it. The next thing I knew she was hovering over my window. Her perfume seeped into Juelz's Range Rover. She smelled real good. Like Cherry Blossom. "Dang, boy, when you get out of Cook County?"

I was as high as a kite, but even under the influence I couldn't deny how fine her lil' caramel ass had gotten. I opened the door to the whip and stepped out. Opened my arms so she could give me a hug.

She hugged me. "Well? When did you get out?"

"If you would have stayed in touch with me you would already know that." I said breaking our embrace and looking down on her.

The light shined off of her forehead. She was fitted in a blue and white Givenchy dress that stopped at the top of her thighs and clung to her every curve. On her feet were black open-toed Gucci pumps. Her toes looked freshly done with their French tips. The wind blew and caused a bit of her hair to go into her face. She pulled it out and placed it behind her right ear. "Damn, TJ, I know you ain't finna come at me like that. Are you?" She tried to hug me again.

I pushed her lil' ass back. "I ain't coming at you like nothin'. You knew where I was, and you only came to fuck with me three times while I was on lock. That shit so fucked up that I didn't even know who you was at first when you rolled up."

She lowered her head. "If it makes you feel any better, I been going through hell ever since you been in there."

"I can't tell. You rolling a ma'fucka Jaguar. Shit can't be too bad for you out here."

She looked at her car and waved it off. "I got my trust fund money. You know my father got gunned down by the police when I was ten years old. Anyway, our family won five million dollars. I got other brothers and sisters on his side. My take home was a lil' less than a million. I been investing ever since I got the money. This whip is just a treat to myself. It don't mean shit to me though. You do."

I jerked my head back. "I do? Really? How the fuck I mean something to you when you only came to see me a few times?"

"Life happens. I may have not came to see you like you feel I should have, but I been thinking about you every single day since you been gone. Now that you're out, I'm willing to do anything for you to prove to you that I'm fucking with you the long way. So, name it, and it's yours."

I looked at her for a long time, trying to think of a way to call her bluff. She looked so good standing in front of me, all thick and shit. I'd never gotten the chance to fuck Punkin, and suddenly I was regretting that shit. "Aiight, you say anything, right?"

"Yep, long as you ain't on no bullshit." She rested her hand on her hip. Then swatted at a fly that flew into her forehead. "Go ahead, I'm waiting."

"Aiight, even though red is my favorite color, I like Raspberry too. Let me get this Jag, and some pocket change." I tested her ass.

She frowned. "Dang, you finna hit me like that?" She looked back at her droptop. Then smiled and stepped into my face. "Aiight, and if I give you this whip, and a lil' change so you can get on your feet, where would that get me?" Her lips brushed against mine.

"Dawg, you better tell that bitch whatever she wanna hear. She finna give yo' ass a whole ass Jaguar. Stop playing!" Juelz hollered out of the window.

"Juelz! Shut up! I don't want him lying to me. I really wanna know where I fit in at?" She rolled her eyes at him, then looked up to me. "Well, TJ?"

I walked past her and pulled open the Jaguar's door. I sunk into the leather seat. Placed my feet all the way under the wheel and closed the door. Adjusted the seat, and the rear-view mirrors. She had a track by Cardi B playing. The bass was nice. It could use a few more punches though. All in all, I had to have this whip. I would change the color of it later is what I was thinking.

Punkin came and rested her elbows on the driver's side window, before coming around to the passenger's side. She sat inside and closed the door. "Tell Juelz you gon' get up with him later. I think that you and I need to spend some time together so we can get acquainted. What you think?" She opened her purse and flashed me a knot of hundreds.

I looked over to Juelz. "Bruh, look, I'm finna fuck with shorty for a minute. I'ma get up with you in a lil' while."

"Don't lie to him. Tell him you gon' get up with his ass tomorrow afternoon sometime. We need to get familiar with each other. I mean that."

"Shorty, you tell 'em." I ordered.

"Shit, no problem." She leaned over me. Her perfume was heavy now. The weight of her leaning over my lap made me get as hard as a rock. "Juelz. He'll see you tomorrow. We on one. Aiight?"

Juelz laughed. "Bitch, you finally finna give me nigga some that pussy after making him wait an eternity?" He cracked.

"Don't worry about what we finna do. He'll get up with you later. Now, bye." She frowned and eased back into the passenger's seat.

I threw up the deuces. "In a minute, shorty." I pulled off and got into traffic. "Yo, throw some Kevin Gates on. Let me roll for a minute."

"Gates? I mess with him a lil' bit. I'ma play that Yukatan from his new album." She switched up the track and allowed for the music to play. She turned it low enough so I could still hear her loud and clear. "TJ?"

I was already nodding. "What's good, shorty?"

"I'm sorry for not staying by your side the way that I was supposed to. I know you fuck with Sodi real tough now. Word is that she been on her game for you. I didn't wanna come in between that. That's my homegirl."

I nodded. "Shorty, you don't owe me no explanation. You did what you did. It is what it is. At least that lets me know how far I can go with yo' ass. That's all."

"What's that supposed to mean?"

"Just what I said. I know if shit get rough that you ain't gon' be there when it all boils down. That just mean that I gotta fuck with you from a distance." Now these were the words that came out of my mouth, but there was no way that I was finna ease up off of Punkin. I was a stick-up kid at heart. Shorty had just told me that she'd gotten an inheritance of just under a million. I didn't know how much under a million meant, but I know it meant more than the lil' $40,000 that I had to my name, so until I was able to hit her pockets I was gon' keep this bitch as close as a shadow. Besides all that, I wanted to see what them guts was about anyway.

"Dang, so what you trying to call me a trifling female or something?" She asked dejectedly.

"If the shoe fits. All I know is that when the nigga tried to take the pussy from you, I got on his ass with no hesitation. I didn't even know you like that, and I was ready to stank his ass. Because of you, this fool still wanna kill me. But you could so easily let me rot in that ma'fucka when you sitting out here with yo' bag all the way up. That says a lot about you. That's just on some real shit."

She nodded real slowly. The sun shined off of her lip gloss. It made her lips look juicy, and succulent. She tended to swallow her spit. Then she covered her face with both hands and broke down crying. This shocked the hell out of me.

"Whoa. Whoa. Whoa. What you crying for?" I asked, shocked.

"Because, you're right. What type of female will let the man who saved her rot? That's so bogus of me. For all I knew, if you wouldn't have saved me that night, that fool could have burned me with that disease that he been giving them other females. You pretty much saved my life, TJ, and I shitted on you. I'm so bogus." She covered her face again, crying her little heart out.

I pulled the Jag to the side of the road and threw it in park. I scanned the streets for any potential jackers, or enemies at all and saw none. Since I didn't, I opted to console her. "Punkin, it's good. Ain't no sense of us dwelling on that small shit. What's done is done. The best thing you can do is to show me how much you appreciate me right now. I'm man enough to wipe yo' slate clean. We're good. You hear me?"

She nodded, then wiped the tears from her eyes. Mascara ran down her brown cheeks. "Well, I am sorry though. I'm willing to make it up to you if I can. You can already have this car. It's completely paid off. I'll switch the title over before you leave. Second to that, I got about fifteen thousand cash on me. You can have that too. All I ask is that you spend the night with me. I just want us to catch up and get to know each other. Is that alright with you?" She sniffled.

For some reason she reminded me of my sister. I saw the vulnerabilities inside of her, and that caused me to soften up just a little bit. I mean, I was still gone hit them pockets, but I didn't see a need to continue to try and mentally manipulate her. It was clear that she held a genuine affection for me. I had to appreciate that. Chicago was a city of cold hearts, and no love. The fact that Punkin harbored some for me was important.

"Yeah. Shorty, we can chill tonight. Just let me get at Sodi." I pulled off into traffic.

"Sodi ain't finna let you fuck with me on that level. She see me as a threat now."

"I thought you just said that she was yo' homegirl?"

"She is. But she ain't finna let me kick it with you all night, TJ."

"Why not?"

Punkin smacked her lips. "Really? You don't know?"

I shook my head. "N'all, I really don't."

Punkin exhaled. "Man, back when we were working at Harold's, I told Sodi that I really liked you. I said the only reason why I couldn't mess with you was because I was already talking to Blue. Blue thought he could control me, and when I didn't follow what he wanted me to do, he always wound up turning violent. I knew that if I would have dropped his ass for you that he would have sent some of his guys off to get at your head on some sucka shit. I couldn't do that. Anyway, when I told Sodi all this, and she saw how fine you were, she pounced. That girl fell in love with you at first sight and she been head over heels ever since then."

"So, why you ain't let me know how you was feeling back then? Or better yet, while I was on lock, why you ain't write me and tell me?"

"TJ, I have wrote that letter so many times. I just never sent it. Like I said, Sodi is my homegirl. Once she got serious about you, I had to fall back. That was the right thing to do." I didn't know if I believed that she'd written that letter a bunch of times, but I didn't feel like dwelling on it.

"So, why you want me to spend a night with you now?" I asked, letting the top up. It was starting to get a bit chilly. I hated being cold. It was cool to roll around in style, but common sense was another thing.

"Because now I just wanna spend some time with you for old times' sake." She blushed and couldn't even look me in the eyes. "I want tonight to be special. We can make it all about you too. That's perfectly fine with me."

"Sounds good to me too." I switched lanes. "Where are you staying now?"

"Harvey, Illinois. The Deep Hundreds." Harvey was like a suburb to Chicago. There were a whole lot of inner-city folk that moved out to Harvey once they started to tear down our Project Buildings, and moved a lot of Section Eight, or rent-assisted programs out to Harvey, and Riverdale, which was another suburb of the city. If Punkin was bagged up like I thought she was, there was no way that she was staying around the rent-assisted areas.

She leaned forward and punched in her address into the GPS system. While she was leaned forward, her dress fell forward and I was able to see down her shirt. Her bra was full of cleavage. The slopes were supple. I could make out a hint of her brown nipple on her left breast. "Here. Now all you gotta do is follow the system. I wanna ask you something too, TJ?"

"What's that?"

"What are you planning on doing now that you're home?"

"I don't know yet. I gotta get my money all the way up."

"And once you do, then what?"

"Then I'ma find out what I wanna do. I know I never wanna go back to jail, ever again. That's for sure. I gotta find a way to make it out of this ghetto. Maybe even this city altogether. It's just that I don't know where I would go if I did. Sodi wanna bounce though."

"Damn, are y'all that serious?" She looked shocked.

I laughed. "Why you say that shit like that?"

"'Cause. You knew me longer than her, and you ain't never expressed feelings about bouncing from this run-down city until now. But at the end of it, you making it seem like it's all her idea, and not yours. So, what's really good?"

I found her getting jealous kind of cute. There it was, that I hadn't talked to Punkin in damn near a year, and she was making it seem like I owed her something. That shit was funny. Now I was back on that hitting her pockets shit.

"Shorty, on some real shit, I'm lost. You already know the shit I done been through with my people. I ain't got a pot to piss in. I can't get serious with nobody until some-body put me up on some green."

"I remember you used to write those books and stuff. Do you still do that?" She asked, placing a tuft of hair behind her ear.

"Why?"

"Because maybe we can put some of your books out there. That will give you a voice. You been through a lot of sadistic shit, TJ. If the world was able to take a glimpse into your life and see what you have really been through, their minds would be blown. They'd probably want them turned into movies. Can you imagine that?"

I could. Making movies was my ultimate goal in life. I loved creating. If I was given the opportunity, I knew I could sit back and write all day long, making one real life movie after the next. "Yeah, I can. But I wouldn't even know how to get started."

"Maybe we can figure that out together. Life is more than the slums. You need to understand that and see yourself as more than a street nigga. You are special, and God put you here for a reason. Now, are you stayin' with me tonight or what?"

Chapter 8

"You should know that the last time we saw each other that I was a lil' shy virgin. But thangs change, TJ." Punkin said, as she stepped out of the bathroom of her bedroom in a sheer purple robe. There were candles lit all around the room. Her shadow danced off of the walls. She stepped to the foot of the bed where I was sitting and opened her robe. Her sexy caramel body seemed to shine in the darkness. She wore a two-piece pink lingerie number. The top pushed her globes nearly out of the cups. She looked like she'd gone up a size in the breast department. Her stomach had a slight bump to it, but I found it sexy. I didn't know many thick ass women that didn't have a bit of a tummy unless they had been under the knife, and in Chicago there wasn't many women in the slums that were able to afford that. Not saying that Punkin couldn't have. My eyes trailed lower to her pink lace panties. They were trapped inside of her sex lips. Her petals were brown on each side of the material. Her lips were thick. "So, I'm saying. What do you think?"

I turned my finger in a circle, motioning for her to rotate in her own circle for me. She did. I saw how the panties were all in her ass. Her big globes juggled on each side of the sunken cloth. Then she was facing me again. "Shorty, what's yo' game plan? Huh?"

She shook her head. "I ain't got one. I just wanna be down with you. I done liked you ever since we were in high school. Now that we're both grown I just thank I wanna put you up on some real shit that extends outside of the hood. You do know that that dope shit ain't gon' last forever, don't you?" She stepped between my legs and crouched. Her hand rubbed over my pants' front. Then she was unhooking the belt and pulling open my jeans.

"So, what you gon' put me up on?" I asked, feeling her fish my dick out.

She stroked me in her hand. Her lips rested against the head. "The new dope game is real estate. I'll pay for you to take some classes down at the Technical College so you can get your license. After you get them, I'll help you buy your first couple properties. What you got to say about that?" She licked her tongue around the tip of my piece, then sucked me into her mouth a few inches. Stroking with her right hand. "Yo' dick so big, TJ. Sodi been taking all of this?" She licked it again.

My eyes couldn't help rolling into the back of my head. I needed for her to quit bringing up Sodi's name though. I didn't need to be thinking about her while me and Punkin were getting down. The last thing I needed was a conscious. I had to fuck Punkin. That shit was long overdue. "Yo, don't bring shorty up. You blowing me right now." I groaned.

Punkin's head disappeared into my lap over and over again. She tightened her lips and sucked me fast and faster. The noises coming from my lap started to drive me crazy. I got to humping upward into her mouth.

She climbed on to the bed and bent over beside me on all fours. Her ass was right next to me face. I saw the way her pussy swallowed up the panties. The sight looked magnificent, and tantalizing. I cuffed her pussy lips. Squeezed them together and grabbed her hips to bring it to my face. Once she was close enough, I pulled her on top of me, and she lowered her panty-covered pussy on to my face. My tongue licked the fabric right away.

"Unn. TJ." She spaced her knees.

I pulled the cloth to the side and exposed her wet gap. Her brown lips were leaking, heavy with her dew. I pulled her down and attacked that pussy like I was starving for it. I still couldn't believe that I was getting a piece of Punkin. She was still like that forbidden fruit. The one girl that I'd always wanted throughout high school, and never got the chance to have. Now here she was laying on top of me, grinding her naked pussy on my lips in heat. The reality was enough to make me cum down her throat. It took every ounce of willpower that I had inside of me to refrain from doing so.

She popped me out of her mouth. "You got a rubber, TJ?" She continued to pull on my piece.

I groaned. "What?" My hips humped upward. I needed her to put her mouth back on me.

"A rubber. If we gon' do anything we need some protection." She sat back on her haunches and rubbed her pussy. Her gash displayed a hint of her pink. Her natural scent rose in the room, mixed with perfume.

I laid on my back for a second longer, then sat up. "Yo, I ain't got no rubber. I ain't been doing shit with nobody but Sodi anyway, and shorty good."

Punkin slid two fingers into herself. She slowly worked them in and out. "And I ain't been fuckin' with nobody either so I ain't had the need for them. Damn. You think we should go out and get some?" She pulled her fingers out of her box and sucked them into her mouth.

It looked so sexy to me. "Fuck that." I climbed onto my knees and leaned over her. "Let me see this ma'fucka for a minute." I rubbed her cat. Smushed the lips together and noted how slippery she was. Then opened the lips and slid my middle finger into her. Her oven felt hot. She moaned and opened her thighs wider.

"So, you think we should risk it? I wanna fuck you so bad, TJ. We are long overdue." She whimpered.

I slipped my face in between her thighs and sniffed that box. Her scent had me feening. "Fuck this." I pulled those pink panties off of her thighs and tossed them somewhere on the floor. My tongue traced her folds. I licked up the salty dew upon them, before sucking each lip into my mouth.

She moaned again. "TJ, please don't get me started. I ain't like these other girls. If we do this, I already know I'ma be a problem over you. Sodi gon' have to compete. She ain't gon' be able to have you all to herself. I'm letting you know that shit right now."

I got on top of her and kissed her lips. I wanted her to taste her own pussy. So, I slid my tongue into her mouth, and sucked on her lips. "You thank you gon' be able to compete with Sodi? Shorty been holding me down ever since you introduced us to each other." I sucked on her neck, and bit into it.

She whimpered and opened her thighs. Reached in between us and pulled out my dick. She squeezed it and placed the head on her lips. Slowly easing me into her wetness. "Ain't nobody more loyal than me. That bitch a bum compared to me. You wanna be up, then you'll fuck with me. You wanna continue to struggle, pulling kick-does and shit. Trapping, and all that other short-term shit, then stay with her. But if you wanna excel, I'm that bitch. Trust that." She slid me all the way into her.

I plunged in and pulled her to me. I whimpered. Her pussy was so wet, and so hot. I couldn't believe the feel of it. I was about to kill that shit when she wrapped her thighs around my waist, stopping me.

"Wait, TJ. Please, hear me out."

"What, Punkin? Come on now." I was rock hard, and deep within her hot womb, thirsty to fuck her with everything that I had.

"I want you to fuck me like a savage, but not the first time. The first time I just want you to sex me like you care about me. Is that too much to ask?" She rubbed all over my chest, and down to my abs.

I looked down into her face and saw how vulnerable she looked. She looked so good to me. Once again she reminded me that she was my high school crush. She was that female that had been off limits. Off limits because of our social status differences. She was a have, and I was a have not. Because of that I had always been afraid to holler at her on that level. But now this bitch was courting me. She wanted to be with me on that level. That made me feel like a boss. Not only because I had her in the palm of my hand, but also because she was a boss bitch. She had that bag. Because she did, there was promise in fucking with her. Promise that I had to capitalize on. "Yeah, baby, it's good. I wanna enjoy this temple anyway. I already know that you ain't the average chick. You deserve a lil' love making.

She rose up on her elbows and kissed my lips. "Thank you, baby. I promise I'll make it worth your while." She wrapped her arms around my neck and pulled me down.

I plunged in and out of her box, slowly deep-stroking her. Every time I plunged, she took a deep breath and shivered. Then she would open her thighs wider to receive me better. As long as I had been fucking, I had never made love until this night with Punkin. It went from me sexing her in slow motion to me gradually building momentum.

She held my waist, and came, digging her nails into me. I played with her clit while I slid in and out of her. Her nipples stood up from her breasts about an inch from the mounds. They were round, and chocolate. Every time I sucked one she would purr. Her pussy felt like it got wetter. I sexed her slowly for a full thirty minutes. After she came the second time, she climbed from under me, and bent over in front of me. "You see all this ass, TJ?" She popped it, and began to twerk in slow motion, making the cheeks jiggled.

"Hell yeah, I do." I stroked my piece, using her juices for lubrication.

"Well, I'm finna let you do everything that you wanna do to me tonight. Ain't nothing off limits. Not only am I finna get your bag right, but I'm finna keep you satisfied in this bedroom as much as I can. I care about Sodi, but she can't fuck in my business. That bitch just convenient, not special." She stretched out on her elbows and laid on her stomach with her ass tooted in the air. "Come beat this pussy up."

I got behind her, and slid in. She yelped. I grabbed them hips and got to fucking her as hard as I could watching my pipe going in and out of her. "Huh. Huh. Huh. Damn. This. Pussy. Punkin. Shit. It's. Good, ma."

She pushed back into my lap, moaning loudly. "Aw. Aw. Aw. Unn. Yes. Shit. Fuck me, TJ. Fuck me. Awwww-shit!" She hollered, and fell back to her stomach, groaning deep within her throat.

I went into overdrive. I slapped that big ass booty, and watched it jiggle like crazy. The harder I smacked it the harder she crashed back into my lap over and over again. The pussy kept getting better and better. "I love this shit!" Pounding. Harder and harder.

She screamed and threw herself back into me and came. Flipped onto her back and pulled me to her with her thighs. She took a hold of my dick, and sunk me right back into her, tossing her calves over my shoulders. I went to work again. "Yes. Yes. Aw-shit. TJ! TJ! I'm cumming! Keep. Beating. That shit up! Please! Please! Awwwww-uh!" She screamed.

Her walls got to gripping me over and over. I couldn't hold back. I came back to back, jerking on top of her. She sucked on my neck and trapped me with her legs. Punkin ran track in high school, so her shit was strong. I kept plunging and skeeting back to back.

She rolled me on my back and pumped my piece at full speed. More of my seed came out of me. She sucked me into her mouth and siphoned like she was hungry for more of my essence.

I cringed and shook on the bed. I made noises that made me embarrassed. She was a genius on the head. I had to give her props. She had me twisting and turning. Then she climbed back up my body, and slid down on to my piece again, riding me like a cowgirl. "This. My. Dick. TJ." Faster and faster. Her titties bounced as she rode me like a jockey.

I held the ass, laid back. The sight of her sweaty dark skin was so attractive to me that I found myself getting lost in it. Her scent. Her sounds. Our heat. All of it became too much. I came again while she rode me.

We flipped over. She wound up curled into a ball. I got to killing her thick ass then. She got to screaming so loud that I wondered if the neighbors in her condo were going to call the police. By the time she came back to back I was exhausted. We fell to the bed breathing hard. I rubbed all over her booty and kept fingering her cat until I fell to sleep.

***

The next morning, I was awakened by a fine ass young Mexican female with long, straight black hair. She had a platter of breakfast food and was setting it on the table just as I opened my eyes. Punkin lay sipping orange juice out of a straw with her laptop on her lap. "Good morning, baby. Yo' phone been ringing like crazy, but I just kept hitting ignore. I think it was Juelz, but I don't know. I didn't look. You hungry?"

I ran my hand over my face and grabbed the phone. I saw that Sodi had been blowing me up all night. I already knew I was in for it. Juelz had hit me up five times telling me to get at him immediately. "Damn. Shorty, why you ain't wake me up?"

"'Cause you looked so good sleeping. Plus, I didn't want you leaving me to go and fuck with whoever was calling you. I ain't ready to be away from you just yet." She said rubbing my chest.

The maid stood there with lust in her eyes. She was about 5'3". Golden complexed with brown eyes, and a gorgeous, strapped body. We made eye contact a few times. Then she looked down at the bed, and blushed.

I'd somehow kicked the sheets off of me and was naked from the waist down. My piece laid along my thigh.

Punkin followed her eyes and smiled. She squeezed it. Just as it stared to grow she covered it back up. "TJ, this is Inez. Inez ,this is TJ. He gon' be staying here from time to time. Come give him a hug."

Inez slowly came over to the bed and leaned over so she could hug me. Her uniform dipped around her cleavage and showed off her globes. She smelled different. Ethnic, but good. She wrapped her arms around my neck. I didn't know her, but it didn't stop me from rubbing all over that ass. She froze at first. Looked over to Punkin. Punkin nodded, then she relented, and slid her hand between my thighs, clutching my piece. "I can't wait to get to know you, TJ." She purred. Kissed my neck, and left the room switching hard.

Punkin laughed and snuggled into the bed beside me. "Like I said before, you'll have more fun with me than you ever would with Sodi. But you'll see. For now, hold me. All I need is another hour of your time, and you can go back to her for a minute. When you come back to me, I'ma put you up on some major cash. Trust me."

I didn't doubt her. I had plans on seeing just what she had up her sleeve. Punkin was spinning a web that I found myself crawling and getting stuck into. Her world fascinated me, and I needed more of it.

T.J. Edwards

Chapter 9

Sodi paced with a mug on her face. Then she stopped. Grabbed the plate of food out of the microwave and placed the dish of enchiladas that she had made in front of me. "Here, nigga, even though I should've dumped this shit in the garbage. I can't believe you stayed out all night and didn't even have the decency to call and let me know what you were up to. What type of shit is that?"

I grabbed a fork and poked at the food. It looked and smelled good, but I didn't know if I could trust her to not have poisoned my shit. I had always heard that Spanish women would do yo' ass in if you fucked them over, so I was worried. "Ma, I was fucked up. I passed out. You know damn well that I just would not have answered the phone. It had to be something else to it." I lied. Looking at the food my stomach got to growling like an angry ass lion. I was about to risk it. I grabbed the Siracha sauce and got to dumping a nice amount on top of them.

"Yeah, right. I know you was laid up with some bitch. It was probably Miss Jackie for all I know because she wasn't answering her phone either. Then when I called early this morning Juelz's irritating ass picked it up. That let me know right there that you were somewhere in the vicinity. But it's good. Just remember that God don't like ugly. Whatever you do foul to somebody, that shit ain't gon' do nothing but come right back around to you." She opened the refrigerator and grabbed a jug of orange juice, followed by a glass. She filled it and set it on the table. "Here."

I was already eating. I didn't feel sick or dizzy yet. So, if she'd poisoned me, I figured I wouldn't feel the effects until after I had already eaten. That would have to suffice. "You bugging, Sodi. Ain't none of these other females out there got shit on you. Ain't no way I'd be fucking off on you. You the only woman I love. That's on everything." I didn't know if I really felt that way about her just yet, but I didn't like hurting her either. After all, she had held me down for eight months as best she could. I knew I was bogus for fucking with Punkin behind her back, but I had a thing for her. Plus, Punkin was bad, and thick as hell. Those were two combinations as a young dude that was hard to ignore. Especially when she was coming at me the way that she was.

Sodi crossed her arms in front of her chest. "Oh, so you love me now?" She stepped closer to the table. "Since when?"

"Since I been feeling that way." I said with a mouthful of food. I swallowed it and grabbed the glass of orange juice. "Why you acting all funny and shit?" I needed to hurry up and try to find a way to turn the tables around on her. You see, the smartest thing to do as a mam when you know that you are in the wrong is to flip the tables and turn the situation around on to your woman. That way it'd fuck with her head a little bit. I needed for Sodi to start second guessing everything that she thought I had done wrong since she didn't have any proof.

"I asked you since when, TJ?" She placed her right hand on the table.

"Yo, you coming at me real foul right now. I made a mistake last night. I drunk too much, and I fell asleep until that shit passed. You know that I don't even drink like that. Juelz had me downing Patron like it was going out of style. Now I got a headache and all kinds of other shit." I took another bite of the food. She did her thing, that was for sure. "The food is good, baby."

"Thank you." She pulled out a chair and sat down. She stared at me from across the table. "Let me smell your dick, TJ."

I dropped the fork. "What?"

"You heard me. I wanna smell your dick. You saying that you ain't been out fuckin' with another bitch. That all you did was pass out after drinking too much with Juelz. Alright, then let me confirm that shit."

I waved her off. "Get yo' crazy ass out of here. What smelling my dick gone do?"

"TJ, I'm Puerto Rican. Nigga, I don't play about my ma'fuckin' man. You finna let me smell your dick so I can calm my nerves, or I'm finna cut that ma'fucka off. Either way, I'm finna get to the bottom of things. You can believe that." She stood up, and pulled a steak knife out of the knife holder. "Now, let me smell your dick."

I finished chewing my food and stood up. I knew that I had showered real good before I left Punkin's house. I'd used half of her body wash and everything. I wasn't worried about Sodi smelling no pussy on me, that was for sure. "Aiight, you really wanna do this?"

"All you did was leave here, get fucked up with Juelz, and come right back home right?"

I nodded. "That's it. I can't believe you don't believe me either. That just proves to me that we ain't got no foundation."

"Nigga, whatever. Bring yo' ass over here so I can get all up in yo' business." She sat the knife on the table.

I stepped in front of her. "You want that ma'fucka, go in there and get it."

She unbuttoned my jeans and pulled them down. She leaned forward and sniffed all over the boxers. Nodded. Then she pulled them down. Grabbed my dick like a flashlight and brought the head to her nose. She sniffed all over it. Pulled the base backward and sniffed it as well. Then she sniffed all under the sack before she grabbed my pipe in her little hand and squeezed it roughly. "Where the fuck did you shower last night, or this morning, TJ?"

I grabbed her wrist. "Shorty, let my shit go. You squeezing it too hard."

"Nigga, answer my muthafuckin question before I pull this ma'fucka off. Where did you shower at?" She asked through clenched teeth.

"I ain't shower nowhere. The last place I showered was here." I lied. Before I had left, me and Sodi had showered together. We fucked right in the shower up against the wall.

"TJ, we used Lever 2000. I know what yo' dick smell like after we use that soap. This ain't no Lever. This smell like some girly shit. What bitch house you been showering over at?"

I was shocked. I didn't know that she could come to a conclusion like that just from smelling me up. I saw that I needed to step my game up when it came to fuckin' with Sodi. She might have been a year younger than me, but she appeared to be lightyears smarter. I smacked her hand away. "You tripping." I pulled my pants back up, and situated my clothes. "Look, I was kind of sweaty, so I wiped down at Juelz's place; that's it. I ain't been fuckin' off with a bitch, if that's what you thinking."

"Nigga, I ain't gotta think nothing. That's what all of the signs are telling me. But it's good. We ain't in a position where we can be one hundred percent faithful to each other. That's duly noted. And as a woman, knowing is half of the battle. Trust me on that." She stood up and ran her fingers through her hair. Her dark curls fell down her back. She stopped at the door to the kitchen and popped back on her legs. Her ass jiggled inside of the white yoga pants that she was wearing. They appeared to be a size too small for her.

I got up, and slid behind her, wrapping my arms around her waist. "Baby, why is it so hard for you to trust me? I really mean it when I say that I love you, girl. Damn."

She allowed for me to keep holding her. That blew my mind a bit because Sodi was so stubborn. "My father cheated on my mother. That shattered her. My brother cheats on his wife all the time. He loves her to death, but he says that he can't help himself. I don't understand men. Nobody ever sat down and took the time to fully break down the psyche for me. All I know is that I refuse to accept anything less than what I deserve from you. Deep in my heart I know that you were with another woman. I feel it." She turned around and looked me in the eyes. "Baby, all I ask is that you keep it real with me. If you will then we can start from scratch. I promise I won't be mad or hold it against you. Were you with another woman all night?"

I didn't know if I could trust her. The last thing I needed was for Sodi to be plotting against me. I still needed her in my corner. I knew there was a thing when it came to women that said they could forgive but they would never forget. That from then on, they would be looking at you from the corners of their eyes. I couldn't deal with that. I already felt like the world was against me for the most part. I needed to know that there was at least one person on the earth that cared about me unconditionally, and that they had my back no matter what. I needed for that person to be Sodi. I couldn't stand to lose her.

"Ma, listen to me." I said, holding her shoulders. "I love you, and I wasn't with another female last night. I didn't fuck off on you. Awright? Now let's move past this."

Sodi looked into my eyes. "Are you serious?"

"Yes, baby."

"Because, TJ, I know you just got out. I can understand that you might wanna fuck a few hoes before you settle down with me. I can understand and accept that. What I can't accept is you lying to me. That would shatter me quick and get me on some vindictive shit. So I'ma ask you one more time. Were you with another female last night? Please be honest, Daddy."

"No, I wasn't. I wouldn't do you like that." As soon as the words left my mouth I felt like shit. I didn't like lying to her. She had given me an out, and I had chosen to still take the low road. I was bogus. I felt terrible.

She nodded. "Okay, TJ. Well, I apologize for coming at you like that. I should have been woman enough to give you more of the benefit than the doubt." She stepped on her tippy toes and kissed my lips. Then stood there looking into my eyes. "And you would never lie to me, right?"

I didn't hesitate. "Never."

"Okay then. Let's move on." She kissed me again, then walked away humming a song to herself. I watched her grab the steak knife. She rinsed it off, dried it, then slid it back into the knife holder before disappearing to the back of the house.

I felt like walking back there and telling her the truth. I felt like apologizing. I didn't want our relationship to start off on the wrong foot. But no matter how much my conscious kicked in, I couldn't do it. My feet wouldn't even begin walking in the same direction of where she was. So, I left it alone. All I had to do was cover my tracks.

T.J. Edwards

Chapter 10

When I told Juelz what had taken place later that night he laughed his ass off. "Nigga, you tripping. If that girl find out that you lying to her, she gon' fuck you over. One thing about them Spanish girls is that they don't play that bullshit. They'll sit back and let you think that everything is all gravy, but all along they been plotting on how to make you pay for whatever it is that you did. You gon' either have to confess to her or start sleeping with one eye open. The choice is yours."

I blew weed smoke into his face. "Shut yo' ass up. You always exaggerating some shit. Shorty ain't gon' get that damn stupid." I was sure.

"Aiight, well I guess we gon' really see now, ain't we?" He snickered, and popped two Xanax pills, chasing them with a bottled water.

I looked to my right and read the sign that said we were now entering into Milwaukee, Wisconsin. "Dawg, where the fuck do you got us at?"

"Shit, I know you done ran through that lil' paper by now. Well, this move here gon' bring us twenty-five bands a piece. After this we can chill for a minute. I got a nice chunk of change put to the side and Jackie talking about helping me to acquire a few properties. I'm on that."

I felt a wave of jealousy go through me. "What's good with you and my old bitch, nigga? Sodi said that when she called shorty this morning yo' lil' shysty ass picked up the phone."

"Shysty? Now why I gotta be all that? Huh?" He asked, with a smirk on his face.

"Answer my question, Juelz, before I piece yo' ass in the jaw." I was serious too. Me and Juelz had fought a bunch of times and the score was damn near even but favoring me. But I was feeling so irritated by his relationship with Jackie that I was sure I could have kicked his ass easily.

"Shorty just a freak. She be on all that taboo shit. Not only that, but she got that paper too. I can't be out here in these streets forever. Sooner or later I'ma have to retire to something smarter and long term. That real estate and exotic clubs is where the real coin is. Property always gon' sell. So will sex. Once I get a few more establishments I'ma leave the streets alone and become an industry nigga. I been fucking around with a few lil' niggas that be rapping and shit. I wanna put they lil' ass in a studio and start recording. Nah mean?" He looked over at me, then grabbed his bottle of water out of the console. He took a swig of it and placed it back. "Besides, you ain't been fucking with that bitch no way. Why all of the sudden you acting like you feeling some type of way?"

"Nigga, I ain't." I lied. "Just feel like you stepping on my toes. When we start fucking with hoes that the other one done already slayed?"

Juelz shrugged. "I ain't even think that shorty old ass counted for anything."

"That's the best answer you got?" I asked dryly. I dumped the ashes into the ashtray and took three more strong tokes of the ganja. My eyes were low as hell.

"Like I said, that bitch is a freak, and she 'bout her paper. It's enough of her to go around. Make her put you up on something. You gotta quit fucking these hoes that can't benefit you once you get from between their legs.

90

That shit old news. It's all about making a bitch elevate you in the game. If all a broad can do is let you fuck, then you walk away with nothing, then you losing, and you've become a loser like her. I don't wanna even see a bitch if she can't elevate me. I only fuck with bosses." He nodded and squeezed his eyelids together. "You remember that one bitch named Mandy? She was Brazilian, and from Miami?"

I shook my head. "You gotta give me more than that. What else?"

"Nigga, I was fucking her that night of Punkin's party in the car. Remember? We were in the backseat, and you and Sodi was in the front."

I thought about it for a minute. "Aw, hell yeah. She was slim, but bad as hell, right?"

"Yeah, nigga, but she ain't slim no more. Not only is she thick as a muthafucka, but she got three strip clubs now. That bitch balling, and guess what?"

"What?"

"She my bitch." He said proudly.

"That's what's up."

"I say that to say that you gotta step yo' hoe game up. If a bitch ain't got no paper, she can keep it moving. The tables have turned. Hoe take care of niggas now. Since that's the case, we gotta capitalize while the getting is good. I'm fuckin' with bad boss bitches only. Know that." He stepped on the gas after looking at the clock on his dash. "Damn, you got me jacking and shit. We got like forty minutes to get to our destination. Two ma'fuckas gotta go down, and we gotta use them tools in the back to do it. Jay say these ma'fuckas gotta be hacked up. I don't know why, but when we done, we gotta bag 'em up, and deliver them to him just like that. Cool?"

"For twenty-five bands, nigga I'll do everything myself. Now let's roll before we late. I can't see myself losing that amount of money for nobody like that."

***

Juelz looked across the table and smiled at me. He threw four more chips into the pile that was already in the center of the table. "I see that four thousand, and I'll raise you four more gees." He held his cards in his hand and eyed the Jamaican that sat directly across from him. "So, what you gon' do homie?"

The Jamaican continued to puff on his fat blunt. Smoke rose to the ceiling from it in a thick rope. "Ya' really tink ya' gonna take me to the cleaners, huh, now boy?" He laughed and added four more thousand-dollar chips to the pile.

The skinny Jamaican to the right of him put his head down and tooted a thick line of pure cocaine. He picked his head up from the table, and sniffed hard, then he retched as if he was going to throw up. He gathered himself. His eyes were watery, and blood shot. "Seems to me that you done met yer match, Radford. This here boy is looking to clean us out. He has guts. I like his style." He said, chopping a razor blade through a pile of pink looking power.

Radford grunted. "Da day a mon comes in me palace and cleans me out is da day I stop being Jamaican. And you know I bleed the black, gold, and green." He sniffed and pulled on his nose. "I call."

Juelz smiled. He waited for a minute then threw his cards on the table. "You got me. I was bluffing."

Radford looked over Juelz's cards. He snickered, then laid out his own cards. "A royal flush. Ma knew you was bluffing, boy." He leaned forward and pulled the pile of chips over to him. His buddy bent down to toot another line.

Juelz nodded as Radford raked the chips up. "Yeah, I guess you did. I see it was easy to read me, huh?"

"I can read any mon, that's why me set to rule Kingston right from here. Everything is in the making."

Juelz nodded. Yeah, that shit sound real slick. Only thang about that is that you like a hundred gees behind on yo' payments to the Dark Souls Cartel. They tracked you all the way here from Jamaica. At least that's what the streets saying."

Radford stopped stacking his chips and sat back in his big chair that looked like a throne. "Ya' wanna run that by me one more time bumbaclot?"

Juelz sat forward and crossed his fingers like an attentive student in class. "The muthafuckin' streets say you in debt, and so does the Reaper." Juelz slammed his hand on the table. "What the fuck you got to say 'bout that?"

Radford laughed, and blew smoke from his nose. "Ya' tickle me, boy. Ya' come here and you act like you're this tough bumbaclot killa. Ma read you now like ma read you in the poker game." He leaned forward, closer to Juelz's face. "You're a fuckin' pussy. I see right through you."

I jumped up with the sawed-off gage in my hands. "N'all, ma'fucka, I see right through you." *Boom! Chick-chick. Boom!*

Two big holes filled his chest. He flew backward in the chair. Then he fell to the ground, shaking and bleeding profusely.

Juelz stood up with two twin Desert Eagles in his hands. He finger fucked them, blasting Radford's guy. The man fell backward as hole after hole filled his body. Juelz stood over his fallen body and continued to fire his gun.

I came and stood beside him, looking around the small one-bedroom apartment. The walls were painted black. They had two red LED light bulbs and that illuminated the entire apartment. I spotted a briefcase on the side of the table. It was the one that Radford had collected Juelz's money, and placed it inside of along with the cash that was already inside of it. "Yo, this where that punk put that cash at." I said rushing over and picking the case up. I kneeled and opened it up. Sure enough, it was stiffed with bills. I closed it back.

Juelz rushed around the apartment closing the curtains. Then he grabbed Radford, and drug him into the kitchen, laying him out on the floor. "Joe, gab that other skinny Jamaican ma'fucka, and bring his ass in here."

I followed his command. "Dawg, you ain't worried about the police being called after all them gunshots?"

"N'all, nigga. This the slum part of Milwaukee. Niggas been busting since we been here." Juelz said, opening his tool pack. He pulled out a mini chainsaw. Pulled the cord, and revved the motor. Then he proceeded to cut off Radford's limbs one by one as if it was the most natural thing in the world. It took him all of twenty minutes, before he had him dismembered. He started on the second man and finished him quicker than he had Radford. When he was done, he stood up wiping the blood from his face.

He took pictures of the scene with his phone, then stepped into the hallway. A minute later I could hear him talking to somebody.

I looked down at both dismembered bodies, lost yet fascinated. I had never seen a body cut up the way that theirs were. I wondered if it had been difficult for Juelz to do. In addition to that, I also wondered if the next time it called for us to fuck somebody over like we had them if he would be cool with me doing what he just had?

Juelz came back into the kitchen looking exhausted. "Come on, bruh. We can leave these ma'fuckas just like this. We got the go ahead. Let's get the fuck out of Milwaukee. I miss the Windy City, baby." The Windy City was what people referred to Chicago as because of its intense windy weather in all four seasons.

"Aiight." I grabbed the briefcase and made my way to the front door behind him. Before he could grab the knob there was a pounding on the door.

Bomp. Bomp. Bomp. Bomp. "Say, Radford, open the doe man or we finna break this bitch down. Ever thang okay in there, Rude Boy?"

Juelz held his gloved finger to his lips. Then, he pointed toward the back door. He tiptoed away from the front door. The banging persisted.

I opened the back door just as the front door came crashing in. I looked over my shoulder and saw three big ass Jamaican-looking ass niggas rush into the apartment. They were armed and looked like they were on business. They must've seen the bodies lying in the kitchen, because the next thing I knew they were busting at us back to back.

I threw the door open and rushed into the backyard. Stopped, and got to bucking back at they ass with the gage. *Whoom! Whoom!*

Juelz fired nine times. We took off running down the dark alley. I was running so fast that I got halfway down the alley and was out of breath. My lungs felt like they were on fire. I gasped for air and kept running.

Boom! Boom! Boom! Boom!

Bullets whizzed past my head. I could actually feel the wind of them. That made me break into my second wind. Juelz was a little way ahead now. We hit the next block and got to the car. He got there first and opened the door as the back window shattered. I said fuck it, and jumped into the back window. I wound up on the backseats. Juelz started up the car and stepped on the gas, speeding away, laughing at the top of his lungs. I didn't see shit funny. I lay there with my heart beating like crazy in my chest. I couldn't get the images of the hacked-up Jamaicans out of my brain. I would see those images every time I closed my eyes for the next two weeks.

Chapter 11

"I know you not used to thinking outside of the dope game, TJ, but this building right here is going to be the first step in you doing exactly that." Punkin said as she took me through a few of the units inside of the apartment building that she had just bought from the city a week prior. It was located on Jarvis on Chicago's northside, right under the El train. It was directly across from a laundromat and cashier's exchange. The apartment building had sixteen units inside of it. Most of them looked like they needed minimal work. Punkin looked over the building with promise. "Like I was saying though. You can charge each tenant eight hundred and fifty dollars a month. Eight hundred and fifty times sixteen is thirteen thousand and six hundred dollars a month. I know it may not be what you're used to but it's a start. I'm putting this first building solely in your name. It's yours. I just wanna see you do better than the dope game. You hear me, baby?" She slid into my arms.

I hugged her, and casually roamed my hands down until they were gripping her ass. She wore a red and black Dolce and Gabbana dress under a matching suit jacket that made her look like a young, sexy businesswoman. Her skin was still so alluring to me. As much as I liked how bad Sodi was, there was still something that drove me crazy about Punkin because of her skin complexion. "I appreciate you, lil' mama. I see what you trying to do for me, and I got mad love for you for it.

"Thank you for saying that, baby. Now, come on. Let me show you around it a little more. I already got a company that's gon' come in and get this bad boy up to code.

It's gon' cost me a lil' penny, but it's worth it. I guess you can consider this a birthday present since you ain't have no party for your actual birthday. Why was that again?"

"I'm having my nineteenth birthday party this weekend. I thought I told you that already."

She shook her head. "Boy, you ain't tell me nothin'. I'm just finding out about this. Where are you having it at?" She asked, looking into my eyes.

I shrugged. "I don't know. I was thinking of having that boy at Sodi's crib. I'm only inviting a few people anyway."

Punkin placed her hand on her hip. "Aw, old girl ain't finna let you do your thing, huh? She too clingy or something?" Punkin laughed and made her way up the stairs.

I watched her ass the entire way. She was strapped. I liked how them ass cheeks seemed to be bouncing into each other. That shit was hot to me. "Shorty ain't on shit. She smooth with it. That's my baby. She keep things light and breezy."

We made it to the third floor. A big ass rat ran past our feet. Punkin jumped up and into my arms. I was laughing like a ma'fucka. I kicked at the rat. It ran down the steps and disappeared. "I guess we gotta call the exterminator too, huh?" Punkin asked. I let her down. She smoothed out her dress and tried to regain her composure. "Well, that was embarrassing."

"That shit was hilarious to me. You done got a lil' bread, and now you acting like you don't know what a rat is. Stop flexing. You was born and raised in Chicago. Everybody in this city know what a rat is."

"First of all, I was born in Gary, Indiana. Secondly, since I been in Chicago, we've been fortunate enough to stay away from the rats and roaches. So, I can't empathize with you there. Buts it's all good though. Anyway, is she gon' have a problem with me helping out with your lil' get together?" Punkin asked, going back down the stairs. I imagined she wanted to get out of the apartment building since she had seen a rat. I still found that funny as hell.

"Why would I need you to help out with my party? What? You think I'm a bum or something?" I knew she was looking for a window to step in and help me out financially, and I was cool with that, but first I had to act all offended and shit.

She stopped and looked back at me. "N'all, baby, I don't think nothing like that. It's just, I wanted to step in a lil' bit to make sure that your day was straight. I mean, it's *your* birthday. That's a big deal for me." She stopped in front of the exit to the apartment building.

I stepped into her face. "Aw, so my day mean that much to you?" My arms slid around her waist. I pulled her to me and kissed her juicy ass lips.

She moaned. "Yeah, it do. I was thinking we have it at one of the beachfront properties my mother got. That way we could chill in a big mansion and go swimming at the same time. She could invite some of my friends. You ever seen how white girls act when they get to drinking liquor and popping pills and shit?" She smiled.

I shook my head. I had never been around a white girl before, so I didn't know how they acted. When I was on lock both times that was all the dudes in there would talk about. I got sick of hearing about them after a while. "N'all, I ain't, but if you feel like you could get some of them to come through then do that. I'ma holler at Juelz and see what he up to."

She stepped forward and kissed my lips again. "That ain't the only person you betta check in with. I think Sodi finna give you all that you can handle. That girl crazy, and she got that Puerto Rican shit in her too. They are way crazier than us sistahs." She laughed. Then her eyes got super big. She jumped up and screamed as a family of rats came out of one of the open apartment doors.

I opened the front door to the building and allowed for them to run outside. When I walked back over to Punkin she was shaking like a leaf. I wrapped her into my arms. "It's all good, baby. We just gon' have to get a good ass exterminator. I'll take care of that on my own."

She continued to shake. "Yeah, you do that. Do whatever you gotta do, and I'll just take care of the bill. Deal?"

"Deal." I wrapped her possessively in my arms. "I been protecting you since day one. You already know I got you. We in this shit together. Right?"

She snuggled up to me. "Right."

"That's all I'm talking 'bout. Now I'ma get everything situated, and you snatch up that beachfront so we can make the dream work. Okay, baby?"

"I got you."

***

Sodi got into the freshly repainted black on black drop top Jaguar that I'd gotten from Punkin with a frown on her face. She closed the door and the seatbelt went across her body. She stopped and sighed. "Whew, what a day."

I pulled away from the curb. "What's good, Mami? How was your day?"

She shook her head and rubbed the right side of her temple. "Horrible. I been having the same migraine since this morning. I feel like I wanna cry." She reported.

"Aw, baby, is there anything I can do for you?" I continued to drive but kept glancing over at her every other second.

"Yeah, you can tell me where you got this whip from." She glared at me, then closed her eyes, still rubbing her temples.

"Punkin. When I first got home, she hit me with it. She said that she felt bad that she hadn't stood in my corner while I was on lock, so she just wanted to do somethin' special for me. Well, this is what she call special, right here."

Sodi kept her eyes closed. "TJ, are you fucking that girl?"

"Man, here we go with this shit. Why we just can't be cool, Sodi, damn."

"Nigga, shut that stupid shit up and answer my question. Are you fuckin' Punkin?"

"Why would you even ask me some shit like that to begin with?" I snapped. I didn't feel like arguing with her this afternoon. There was only two days until my birthday party. I wanted to be in a good state of mind.

"Because ever since you came home that girl been acting real funny. She ain't been hitting me up on Facebook like she usually did. She don't text me, and the bottom line is I can tell when a bitch is up to no good. Now answer my question. I need to know if you are fucking her."

"Sodi, you tripping. I ain't about to go there with you. I know that all you're looking for is a fight because she bought me this new whip. I get it, but it ain't even that serious."

"Aw, so once again you gon' leave me to come to my own conclusions, huh?" She nodded. "Nigga, aiight. That's cool."

"Ain't no ma'fuckin' conclusions to come to. It's just a whip."

"Boy, ain't no bitch finna give you a Jag just because she feeling some type of way about not holding you down for whatever reason. I ain't stupid, and I know what you got between your legs. That's what that bitch gave you this car for, ain't it?" She looked over at me with her eyes squinted. I could tell that the migraine was really fucking with her.

"Man."

"Aw shit, baby, there go JD punk ass right there." She pointed out the windshield.

I followed her finger until I saw my brother JD. He was just getting into a cherry red Bentley truck. A white girl opened the passenger door to his whip and got inside as well. I felt my heart pounding in my chest. I slid the .9 from under the seat and placed it on my lap. All I could do was hear my sister's voice in my head from the last time that we'd spoken on the phone and she was saying that she feared that JD and my father Kalvin was about to do something tragic to her. My heart felt like it was breaking all over again. Then I remembered the conversation that my mother and I had had on her death bed. Her dying wish was that I protected my sister. That I made sure that she was well taken care of at all times. I had failed her. I had failed both of them. I felt like shit. But now I had spotted JD. I frowned, and a cold chill went down my spine.

"Honey, what are you thinking?" Sodi asked, grabbing her purse and taking out a .9 millimeter. It had a pearl white handle on it.

"Where the fuck you get that from?" I asked, pulling off in traffic behind JD's truck.

"My brother gave it to me. You already know how deadly Chicago is. Everybody gotta be strapped around this ma'fucka." She cocked it and looked over to me. "So, what we finna do?"

"I'm finna roll up on this nigga and ask him what happened to my sister. If he say anything stupid, then I'm blasting his ass." I meant that.

"What about that redheaded bitch in his passenger's seat?" Sodi asked, leaning all the way back. "You want me to take care of her for you?"

I looked over to Sodi with new eyes. "Shorty, you making it seem like you down with murdering something. Is that the case?" I wanted to know the truth to that because if she was, I had plans for her lil' ass like right away. There was nothing more attractive to me than a woman who was down to bust her gun beside her man on some ride until the death type shit.

"I'll do anything for, and about you, TJ. The sooner you learn that, the better off we will be. Trust me on that. Let's go holler at them. You take care of JD, and I'll handle her if it comes down to that. Okay? Don't we need like a mask or something?"

Now I was really shocked. "We'll see. For now, let's just play this shit by ear. I stepped on the pedal.

"Aiight, let's roll then." She said digging through her purse. She took out a pair of stockings and small scissors and got to cutting away. "I never told you this before, TJ, but I know how you get down in the street. I know you done snuffed more than a few people. But I ain't so innocent either." She stopped cutting and looked up at me.

"What you mean?"

She went back to cutting up the stockings. "Well, my mother had this boyfriend that had a habit of kicking her ass for no reason. He was a drunk. A real loudmouth, disrespectful ma'fucka. And let's just say that one day he beat my mother too long, and I got sick of it. After cleaning her up, I helped her into her bed, then I went into her bedroom closet. I took my daddy's gun and waited until Mark had to go the liquor store. You see, he did this every single night thirty minutes before the liquor store closed. Anyway, this particular night I followed his ass through an alley on Fifty-Third. He was on his way to the liquor store that was right on the corner of Ashland. I waited inside of a garage that he walked past on his route. It was in the alley that led away from our projects. On his way back he stopped in the middle of the alley and opened his bottle of Jack Daniels. As soon as he did, I stepped out of the garage with my daddy's gun aimed at him.

"He stopped stanking long enough to see that it was me. After he confirmed that it was, he laughed and began stanking from the bottle again. He said, 'Lil' girl, if you don't put that fake gun down and go find you somebody to play with, I'ma kick yo' monkey ass. Now, try me.' Tears fell down my cheeks. I had never even shot a gun before, but my daddy had shown me how, what seemed like a million times. I stepped in front of him. 'Mark, I'm tired of you beating on my mother. It has to stop.' He twisted the cap back on his Jack Daniels. 'Lil' girl, I'm a grown ass man. You don't tell me what I best be doing.

You need to stay in a child's place.' He stepped toward me. 'Stop pointing that damn toy in my face.' I backed up. 'Stay back. It's not a toy. I swear to God I will kill you. I'll leave you right here in this alley.' He said, 'Oh yeah? Well, we finna see about that.' He rushed me. I panicked and aimed the gun. I kept squeezing the trigger on the .357 but it wouldn't fire. Finally, before it was too late, I remembered the hammer. I cocked it back just as he closed in on me. Then fired. Boom. The bullet smacked him in the center of his forehead. I will never forget how he looked so stunned. He dropped his bottle of liquor first. It didn't break. Then he fell to his knees with his forehead wide open. He lay there in a puddle. As soon as I killed him, I started to panic. I turned to run away from the scene and ran smack dab into somebody from our school. Luckily, he was cool. He helped me get rid of the body. That night I wound up getting drunk for the first time off the Jack Daniels that I had gotten off of Mark. So yeah, I ain't new to this killing shit. I wish I was, but I'm not. This is Chicago after all." She looked out of her window. "I have never told nobody that story either. Nightmares of him still haunt me."

"Well, yo' secret safe with me, boo. Fuck that nigga. That's why I wanna get up with JD glamour right now." My brother pulled into an underground parking garage to an apartment complex. I followed him with my heart really pounding. Sodi's story had gotten me riled up to say the least. I knew she would bust her gun, and that was motivation.

T.J. Edwards

106

Chapter 12

I pulled the Jaguar right to the side of JD's truck just as he was getting out. Rushed him. He'd opened his driver's door, and tried to rush back into it, but it was too late. I had one hand wrapped around his neck. The other held my pistol that was placed to his temple. I had chosen to wear the stocking mask over my face. I watched Sodi slide through the truck with her gun out. She snatched up his redheaded passenger.

JD frowned and held his hands at shoulder level. "Fuck you want, nigga? If it's the truck, gone 'head and take that ma'fucka. It's light work. I got ten gees on me and that's it. Take that shit and go."

Inside of the truck I could hear the redhead screaming. There was a slapping sound. Then she was quiet. Sodi's voice was muffled, but she seemed in control of the situation.

I cocked the hammer and pressed it harder to JD's temple. "What happened to Marie, nigga?"

JD's eyes got big. "What? Who the fuck is Marie?" He asked, acting dumb.

I tightened my grip. "Nigga, you know who the fuck Marie is. What happened to her? Which one of you bitch ass niggas killed her, and tossed her into the trash?" I asked, ready to pop his top like a pill bottle.

"That shit ain't got nothing to do with me. I don't know who killed her, and to be honest with you I really don't give a fuck. Life goes on."

"Yeah, nigga, that's how you feel. You think a ma'fucka can take my sister life, and shit just goes on as usual?" I placed the gun to his neck.

He swallowed. "TJ. So, you finally home, huh?"

"Yeah, nigga, I'm home, and yo' bitch ass finna tell me what happened to my sister." I stuffed his ass back into his truck. I don't know what had taken place with Sodi and the white girl, but the redhead was knocked out cold, lying flat on her back in the back of his Bentley truck. "Baby, keep yo' pistol to the back of this nigga head. We finna go for a lil' trip. He gon' tell me what the fuck I need to know about Marie, or I'm finna send his ass to the reaper."

Sodi slammed her barrel to his neck. "Bet those. With his sick ass. I heard what y'all was doing to that girl. We should cut his ma'fuckin' dick off, then find the other two and make they ass eat it until they puke." She snapped.

She was definitely speaking my language. I threw the truck in reverse and pulled out of the parking garage on my way back to the northside. I had plans for JD. Before it was all said and done, I was going to get my answers from him. I didn't give a fuck what I had to do.

***

Juelz stepped into the basement and started laughing as soon as he saw how me and Sodi had tied JD's ass up. We used duct tape and it didn't look the neatest. I think we went a bit overboard. JD looked like he was getting pre-pared to sit in the electric chair. Juelz stopped in front of him and kneeled. "Damn, you in a fucked-up position, homeboy." He took the book bag off of his shoulder that held the utensils I looked forward to using on JD to get answers out of his ass. He tossed it to me, and I took them out.

JD looked like he was trying to break his binds. He groaned into the duct tape. Sweat rolled down the side of his face. There were specks of blood leaking from a cut under his right eye. Sodi popped him one good time for all women's sake, as she called it.

Juelz walked over to her and gave her a hug. They said something to each other in Spanish. She nodded and he hugged her again. "So, what you finna do to this bitch ass nigga, TJ?"

I took out a tool that had a handle like a screwdriver, but an end like an icepick. I stood up and walked over to JD. "Look, bruh, I don't wanna do this shit to you." I lied. "All I wanna know is who killed Marie. You tell me that and you gon' make shit lighter on yourself." I ripped the duct tape from his mouth. "What happened?"

He hollered as loud as he could, over and over again. I laughed at his stupid ass. For one, the El grain was screeching by on its tracks. Secondly, we were in the basement of the building that Punkin had just given to me so there was nobody inside of it other than us, and the redhead who was also duct taped to her chair. So, I wasn't worried about being disturbed, or how loud he hollered. In fact, the louder he hollered the more it would excite and encourage me.

Sodi stepped up to him and smacked him so hard that he spat blood across the hot water heater. "Shut all that ma'fuckin' hollering up. You sound like a little bitch. I bet you wasn't making all that noise when you were doing what you were doing to her, was you?" She spat.

JD shut up. He mugged Sodi. "Bitch, if you ever put your filthy Spick hands on me again, I'ma eat yo' ass one bite at a time," he hissed.

She placed her hand on her hip. "Oh, really?" She yanked the icepick out of my hand and waved it in his face. "So, what you gon' do if I use this? Huh? You still gon' eat me bite by bite if I stab this ma'fucka in here!" She raised it and slammed it into his knee as hard as she could. The icepick sank into his flesh nearly to the handle.

Before he could holler, I slapped the tape back across his mouth. He roared behind it. He shook in his seat and threw his head back in obvious pain. His eyelids squeezed together, then he opened them. Tears spilled down his cheeks.

I ripped the tape back off. "What happened to my sister?"

He continued to shake. His eyes slowly made their way over to me. "You gon' let this punk bitch do this to me? I'm yo' ma'fuckin' brother. We got the same mother, and the same father. This punk bitch ain't no kin to us. What's wrong with you!" He snapped. Boogers aligned his top lip from him breathing so hard.

I kneeled. "What happened to my sister, JD?"

Sodi came and yanked the icepick out of his knee. She stood beside me, mugging him with pinned up hatred. Her and Marie had established a bit of a bond. I could tell that she cared about my sister. That made me feel some type of way about her.

Juelz pulled out a bag of Flaming Hot Cheetos. He opened them and began crunching loudly. "You better tell them what's good. This shit can't get no better for you, homeboy." He shook his head and started eating some more of them.

JD mugged him. "Nigga, I could've smoked yo' ass on more than one occasion, but I let you live. I let you keep that punk ass air in your lungs because I ain't have nothing against you. You need to tell this nigga to let me go, Juelz. Tell him to end this charade. My bitch pregnant over there. She five months out from having my seed. "

Juelz kept crunching. "This shit ain't got nothing to do with me. This some family shit right here. Bruh gon' do what he gon' do? I can't stop him from handling his business." He wiped his mouth with his hand. "Far as you letting me live." He laughed. "Boy, I bet you regretting that shit now."

I stood and smacked JD across the face hard. "Bitch nigga, what happened to my sister?"

He looked up at me. "That bitch dead, that's what happened to her. And nigga, you gone be too once Deion and the Moes get a hold of yo' ass. You thank shit sweet. The bounty on yo' head done went from fifty thousand to a hundred thousand. That nigga want you so bad that he willing to drop them chips." He sniffed blood back into his nose. "So, you can kill me, but real soon you gon' be joining me." He laid his head back. I watched blood ooze out of the icepick wound in his knee.

Sodi stepped forward. "You want me to inflict some more serious pain to his ass?"

I stepped back and nodded. "Yeah, boo. Slam that ma'fucka in there and twist that bitch over and over. This nigga think he tough."

She shrugged. "Will do." She stepped forward and looked like she aimed for the same hole. She slammed it into his knee and twisted it in a grinding-like fashion.

JD gritted his teeth. Sweat dripped off of his chin. "Get this bitch away from me, TJ! Awww!" He said through his pierce screaming. He sounded like a bitch.

Sodi kept twisting and twisting. By the face she was making I could tell that she was putting her all into it. She yanked it out. It was dripping in blood. "Again, Daddy?"

"Hell yeah." Juelz said amped up.

Sodi kept looking at me, ignoring him. "He think he so tough, we need to really torture his ass."

Juelz dropped his bag of chips. He rushed over to the bag and pulled out a blow torch. "Bruh, you get to burning this nigga, I guarantee you find out what happened to your sister."

"I'll do it." Sodi announced, walking over and grabbing the canister from Juelz.

I snatched it from her. For just a split second, a moment of protectiveness came over me for JD. He was still my brother, and I didn't want them ganging up on him. If anybody was gon' make him feel some intense pain it should have been me, and I decided right then that it was going to be me. I started the torch. "Look, JD, shit about to get real ugly, lil' bruh. All you gotta do is tell me who killed Marie and how it happened. I need closure." I brought the flaming torch close to his face.

"Nigga, I don't give a fuck what you do. I'ma take my shit like a man. Fuck you and Juelz, and fuck that Spanish bitch. All three of you ma'fuckas can kiss my Black ass. Now handle yo' business. Fuck that flame."

I brought it to his face and watched his skin melt away. First it turned black. Then it split and began to bubble up. The next thing I knew there was a hole there, and blood was running out of it like a blob.

JD closed his eyes, but he didn't holler. He surprised me that he had gained so much heart. My brother had always been the weakest out of the boys in our family. So,

I was impressed, yet determined to make his bitch ass fold.

"Aiight, nigga. I see what it is." I handed the torch to Sodi and turned JD's chair so that he was facing his baby mother. "Shorty, I want you to go over there and give that Snow Bunny the business. Make this nigga feel something."

"My pleasure." She took the torch and stepped in front of the redhead. "Bitch, do you know what happened to my man's sister? Huh? JD ever talk about it after sex, huh?" Sodi ripped the tape off of her mouth.

She shook her head. "No, I swear. I don't know anything. Please. He's just the father of my child. I don't know anything about the hood. I swear it."

Sodi looked back and laughed at me. "You hear this bitch? She don't know nothin' about the hood." She mocked her.

"'Cause she don't! Bitch, leave my lil' hoe alone. She ain't got shit to do with this." He tried to break free of his binds again. The scent of his cooked skin was heavy in the room.

"Well, nigga, you already know how this shit go in Chicago. Birds of a feather. If you're my enemy, then yo' bitch is too." Sodi began searing the side of the redhead's face with the flame. The basement began smelling like burned bacon. She kept going. A huge smile spread across her face.

The redhead screamed loudly. She shook against her binds now. Pissed on herself. Sodi kept burning. She screamed, and threw her head back, bleeding profusely.

Sodi stepped back and looked over to me. "Well?"

I winked at her. Then I was back in front of JD. "This shit gon' only get worse."

"Allah, Father of the Universe. Father of love, truth, peace." JD began.

"Fuck he doing?" Juelz asked, stepping beside me.

"He's saying the Moorish prayer. This nigga preparing to die." I said defeated.

"Well, kill his ass then. Ain't no other way around it." Juelz returned.

I looked down on JD as he prayed. Flashes of our childhood came back to me when we were just little innocent kids living in the Cabrini Green Housing Projects. At one point in time we were close. We had each other's backs. Then the years later would change all of that. He started to look up to a callous Deion. Approved of my father beating my mother like crazy, and he became equally disrespectful to her. Worst of the worst he began desiring Marie. That's when shit got crossed, and I began to hate him, and no longer saw him as my blood.

I took the Navy Seal knife out of the bag and took a deep breath. "Yousa a bitch ass nigga for what you did to my lil' sister. I don't know if you're the one that actually killed her, but you deserve to die just the same."

He kept praying, repeating the same prayer over and over. "Allah is my Protector by day and by night through his Holy Prophet, Noble Drew Ali."

I was disgusted. Now that nigga wanted to run to religion. "Yousa clown."

Juelz scooted the redhead in front of him and stood behind her with a blade of his own. "You should have killed me when you had the chance, JD." He slid the blade from one of her ears all the way across to the next. It opened up like a mouth. Then her lap was full of blood. She started to choke.

I slipped behind JD before I could allow my thinking to prevent me from doing it. I sliced his throat from one ear to the other, the back again. His hot blood drenched my fist. I kept cutting over and over again, imagining him on top of Marie. I saw him hurting her. I saw her crying, and I kept slicing until both Sodi and Juelz pulled me off of him. By that time my fist was inside of the opening in his throat, and I had still been cutting.

"Dawg, that nigga dead. Let's chop these ma'fuckas up and move on. You wanna find out what really happened to your sister, you gon' have to get yo' hands on Deion." Juelz said, taking the bloody knife from my hand.

Sodi kissed my cheek. "It's all good, Daddy, we gon' get 'em all. You betta believe that."

T.J. Edwards

Chapter 13

I profiled in front of the mirror a few days later in a raw ass black and gray Chanel fits with the matching Retro Number Six Jordan's. My neck was dripping with three chains and a custom TJ piece that was drenched in diamonds. Once again it had been another gift from Punkin but I ain't tell Sodi that. She was already feeling some type of way because Punkin was throwing my birthday bash at her beachfront estate. I didn't know if it was hers or her mother's, but either way I was about to kick it. I had plans on getting fucked up too. I had already told Juelz that I needed him to watch my back.

Sodi came into the room in a gray and black Givenchy dress. She had her long, curly hair in a ponytail falling down her back. She rocked a black Chanel hairbow that made her look like a lil' girl. Her make-up was flawless, and she had her toes out. They were painted to match her fit. She looked good as a muthafucka. She slid behind me as I was spraying a bit of cologne on. "Damn, Papi, you looking good as hell. I don't think I want you in a party full of bitches tonight. Let's just stay in."

I turned around with my face balled. "What make you think you the only one deserving to see a boss?" I turned back around and looked into the mirror.

"Aiight now, don't get yo' ass slumped. You can do yo' thing, tonight but remember that you still belong to me. You got that?"

"Shorty, when you look this good, you can't belong to no one woman. Are you kidding me?" My dreads were freshly twisted and shining. I could see my parts and everything. I looked crispy. I had my face lined up and smelled good. Yeah, I couldn't wait to hit up my own party.

Sodi reached into her purse and brought out the Glock .40 that I had given her. "Nigga, you think I'm finna play with yo' Black ass, huh?"

I laughed. "You shoot me then you lose a boss ass nigga. That's gon' be yo' fault. Can't no ma'fucka out here duplicate me."

She frowned and put the gun away. "Daddy, why are you playin' with me? You got me feeling insecure and shit. You ain't finna go to this party looking for another bitch, is you?" She stepped into my face with her bottom lip poked out.

I smiled and sucked on that ma'fucka. "Never that. Can't nobody do me like you can, Mami. You know you're my world."

She smiled. "I better be." She rubbed all over my chest, looking into my eyes with her light brown ones. I always found myself getting a lil' lost whenever I peered into them. Sodi was already fine as a muthafucka, but her natural light brown eyes seemed to take her to the next level for me. "Daddy, I want you to have a really nice time. Just remember what you mean to me and honor the bond that we have. That is all I ask." She hugged me.

I hugged her for a second, then backed her away from me so I could make sure she didn't wrinkle up my clothes or something. I needed to be fresh for my party. "I got you, boo." I gave her a slight peck on her lips and went back to getting myself together in the mirror.

She stood there looking at me with her arms crossed in front of her. "Nigga, I swear to God, on everything I love. I'd kill a bitch over you, TJ. I ain't playing either.

118

You got me so ma'fuckin' in love with yo' ass that I would literally kill a female over you. You belong to me. Now play with shit tonight if you want to and you gon' find yourself, and whoever else, in a sticky position. You got my word on that." She grabbed some perfume off of her dresser and sprayed it a few times over her body. Then she left the room.

I wasn't paying Sodi no mind. It was my birthday celebration. I was all caught up on me. It was the one day out of the year where I could be on some self-absorbed shit, and that's exactly what I was on.

***

I don't know where Juelz got it from, and I didn't even care. But he pulled up to Sodi's place an hour later in a red Hellcat. Lifted the doors and jumped out of it fitted in a black and red Gucci fit, with the matching Number Four Retro Jordan's. We were Chicago niggas. Even though we rocked designer clothes, most of the true street niggas from Chicago always kept shit real by busting a pair of Jordan's to complement their apparel. Juelz and I were no different. My retro Jordan's had little Chanel symbols all over them though. I felt like I was really fucking the game up.

Juelz walked up to me and handed me the keys. "Here, nigga. This is a rented gift from a friend that I'ma introduce you to when the time is right."

I grabbed the keys and looked past him. I couldn't believe that this fool had actually pulled up in a Hellcat. I got into the car, for a second looked around at its spaceship like dashboard and nodded. "This what I'm talking about right here, homie." I got out and hugged him, just as Sodi came down the stairs looking like a perfect God-dess. Her curly hair bounced behind her. Before she even made it beside me, I could smell her expensive perfume.

Juelz placed his fist to his mouth. "Damn, Sodi, you look bad as a muthafucka." He nodded. "Hell yeah. That's that Rican shit right there."

She laughed. "Back on up, nigga, I belong to TJ. Gone find you a bitch that's a few notches below a Queen. You feel me?" She slid her arm around my lower waist.

Juelz laughed. "Yeah, aiight. I don't give a fuck what you talking 'bout. Bruh finna be dancing with plenty hoes tonight. You definitely finna save me a dance."

She rolled her eyes. "Whatever, Juelz."

A cherry red Porsche truck pulled up with tinted win-dows. It came to a halt so fast that I would up upping both of my Desert Eagles, ready to air that bitch out. The worst thing about having so many enemies was that every car that rolled past, or stopped directly in front of you tended, to spook you. I had chill bumps all over me, and both safe-ties on my guns popped off.

Juelz threw up his hand. "Whoa. Whoa. Whoa, bruh. That's the Brazilian Mandy from school. I told you shorty was having that big bag now." He walked over to her truck, and she rolled down the window. I was only able to see a little bit of her face, but from what I saw, shorty was still killing shit. The Brazilian bitch was bad.

Sodi stepped into my line of vision. "Come on, Papi, let's get the fuck out of here."

***

When I stepped into the party, Punkin was there wait-ing with two gold bottles of Moët. She handed them to me and gave me a hug. "I'm so glad that you finally made it, baby. I been missing you." She whispered.

I hugged her, and knew I had to play it cool since Sodi was only a few paces back. "Yo, I appreciate you, boo. This ma'fucka rocking already. Who is all these people?" I asked looking around at the crowded mansion. I saw females walking around the party so tall that they didn't have any other choice but to have been models. They were of all races, and fine as hell.

"These are a lot of my professional friends. There wasn't a bum invited to your party. Everybody here has their own things going on, and they are successful in their own right. Hobnob, get to know some people. Everybody here can be used as a positive crutch in whatever you are trying to pursue in life." She took a step back and looked past me. "Sodi, hey, girl. Damn you killing that Givenchy."

Sodi smiled. "Thank you, Mami, you know I'm trying. This one right here be keeping me on my toes. He think he the shit." She quipped.

I picked a piece of lint off of my fit and adjusted my chains. "Thinking and knowing is two different thangs. I'm finna go fuck with some of these white girls. I'll check with y'all in a minute." I laughed walking off.

"TJ, don't get yo' ass killed! I ain't playing either!" Sodi yelled.

I heard her but kept it moving. I slipped into a section where there were three bad ass white girls that looked like models. They were sipping from their Apple Martini's and dancing to the Megan Thee Stallion she had banging out of the speakers. I held up the two gold bottles. "Yo, I'm TJ, and this is my party. I wanna dance with all three of you." They looked at each other and laughed. They kept dancing as if they thought I was playing or something, but I wasn't. "Yo, I'm serious." I moved between the trio.

One had dark black hair, and bright blue eyes with a nice figure. She handed her drink to her buddy, then came in front of me. "TJ, you're jacked. You just workout a lot?"

I pulled her to me, and we got to grooving. I handed the bottles off to her blonde friend and got to feeling all over her ass while we danced to the music. Luckily it was dark enough for me to do my thing. Her short skirt rose. My hands went under it until I was rubbing on her hot flesh. When my fingers played over her naked pussy, she leaned forward, and kissed my neck. "Mmm, I like dancing with you." I slipped two fingers up her box and got to doing my thing.

Her other blonde friend came up behind me and kissed my neck. She humped into the back of me. Reached around us, and took a hold of my piece, squeezing it. "Damn, you strapped. You do Mollie? Let's take this back to our condo. It's ten minutes away from here." She announced, sucking on the back of my neck.

My fingers were going full speed in and out of her friend. She was moaning and humping into them. Her nipples were hard enough for me to be able to make them out through her white dress that she wore without a bra. Her friend had me so hard that I was ready to fuck. I closed my eyes and sucked all over her neck. When I opened them, I saw Sodi making her way across the room. That caused me to panic. I didn't know if she could see all that I was doing, or if she was simply coming in the direction because she was looking for me. Either way, she had me feeling prepared for some drama to kick off. Before she could make it halfway to me, Juelz slipped from the crowd, and slid his arm around her neck. She paused at first, looking up to see who it was. When she saw that it was him, she began talking, probably asking him if he knew where I was because he shook his head. Then he guided her out to the dancefloor. She reluctantly followed him, scanning the crowd for me.

The female with the white dress whispered into my ear, "Baby, so what are you thinking? You wanna come back to our place and take this thing to the next level? We got Mollie and all kinds of coke." She kissed my cheek. "You ever been with super models before?"

I could feel her friend licking all over my neck. She squeezed my pipe through my pants. I was about to find a way to take both of their asses down right there at the party because I had never been with a white girl before, when Punkin slid beside us, and grabbed my wrist.

"Sorry, ladies. This one is off limits." She pulled me out of the crowd, and into a dark hallway. There were two big security guards standing on point. We went past them a few paces. "Y'all, don't let nobody come down this hall-way." She ordered.

They nodded and went back to watching over the party. They looked like two big ass football players. Both were bald with huge arms.

When we got into the hallway, she pushed me up against the wall, and tongued me down, moaning into my mouth.

I gripped that fat ass. She was wearing a short, all-pink Fendi skirt dress. The material was thin enough for me to feel how hot she was under it. I sucked on her neck, and bit all over it.

"TJ, baby, you gotta fuck me for ten minutes. Come on. Just give me ten minutes of this dick then we can slip back into the party like ain't nothing happened." She grabbed my wrist again, and ran down the hallway with me, and up a spiral case of stairs.

We busted through the door of the first room that we came to. Punkin yanked up her dress, and pulled her bikini panties down, and off of her ankles. Then she bent over the bed, spacing her feet. "Come on, TJ."

I set both pistols on the bed. Dropped my pants and fingered her fast and hard from the back until I was sure she was wet enough to take me. Then I slid in. Her lips seemed to slurp me inside of her. I entered into her wetness and got to fucking her like my life depended on it.

Punkin gripped the blankets on the bed and balled them into her fists while she bounced back into my lap, faster and faster. "Unn. Unn. Awww. Yes. TJ. Mmm. Mmm. TJ. Fuck me, bay-beeeee-a." She slammed back with brute force and came in the first three minutes.

I kept stroking. I couldn't keep my eyes off of her jiggling booty. That ass was juicy, and hot. My piece kept separating her thick lips. Every time I would pull out it seemed as if I was lubed with more of her juices. They excited me and made me pound that pussy harder and harder. When I dug my nails into her hips, she screamed. I came shooting jets all into her womb.

She must have felt them because she shivered, and kept bouncing back, milking me. "Unn, I love you, TJ. Fuck." She wiggled from under me, and dropped to the floor, taking me into her mouth. She sucked me while looking up at me. Her head bobbed into my lap. She pulled me out with a loud sucking noise. "You drive me crazy, you know that?" More sucking. Her tongue wrapped around the head. Then her eyes were closed while she sucked with full speed.

I balanced myself on my feet. Held the back of her head, and slowly rocked back and forth into her mouth. It felt so good. I took three steps back and dislodged my piece from her lips. Kneeled, and picked her ass up. We crashed into the wall. I got to bouncing her. Fucking that tight pussy. It felt like a wet fist, squeezing me. She licked all over my neck. Moaned at the top of her lungs and dug her nails into my shoulder blades while I wore her thick ass out. Then, somehow, we fell to the carpet. Once there, I really got to stroking, digging as deep into her box as I could.

She pulled me down, and came, screaming. "You're killing me, TJ! Aw shit! Yo' dick too deep! It's too deep! Aww-fuck!" Her eyes rolled into the back of her head.

The sight was too much. I could feel her womb contracting. I came back to back. All in her box, sucking roughly on her neck like a savage. By the time I came from between her thighs, I was exhausted and ready to call it a night. When I got back outside to the party, Sodi was nowhere to be found. I figured she'd gotten tired of looking for me and bounced. I felt bad, but Punkin's pussy had a hold on me to say the least.

Chapter 14

I didn't run into Jackie until two weeks after my birthday. Me and Sodi were on bad terms because of what had taken place at my birthday party two weeks prior. We were speaking the bare minimum to each other. We never really discussed what had taken place that night. She didn't ask me where I had been. And I didn't ask her why she left, or how she got home. We just left the shit alone.

I was out rolling around in the Jaguar on my way to get a box of blunts when a platinum G Wagon pulled behind me and got to blowing its horn. I already had a Tech .9 on my lap with fifty in the clip, anxious to use it because I woke up on the wrong side of the bed. I pulled to the side of the street, and Jackie pulled up beside me. She rolled down her tinted window and smiled, with her hair whipped. She looked like she had aged just a slight bit, but her dark skin looked good none the less. I felt some sort of an emotional attachment to her as soon as I saw her face.

"Aw, so yo' lil' ass get out of jail and you don't even think about coming to see me, huh?" She asked, now looking serious.

I smacked my lips. Even though she had me feeling some type of way, I wasn't about to let her on to that shit. Nor was I going to give in to her charms so easily. "I thought you'd be somewhere fucking my right-hand man. Fuck all that's about anyway?" I asked sounding like a sucka.

She frowned. "Boy, wait a minute. I'm 'bout to pull over and holler at you for a minute." She rolled the G Wagon up ahead and parked in front of a parking meter.

Got out and filled it with a bunch of quarters. Then she took her time walking all sexy like to my passenger's side. Jackie had gotten thick as hell. I had to admit that. She looked like she had a bit of a gut, but it looked good on her. I didn't think a female could get thick anyway without having a slight stomach. I found that shit hella sexy, so I couldn't help physically lusting for her old ass.

She stopped and stood in front of the door like something was wrong. She cleared her throat. "Ahem!"

I mugged her and popped the locks. "It's open. Fuck you waiting on?"

She jerked her head back, then bent down. "Boy, if you don't get yo' monkey ass up out this car and open this door for me, I know something."

I sat there for a minute on some rebellious shit. Then I pushed open my door and slid out. I stood beside her, eyeing her with a slight mug. Bumped her out of the way and opened the door for her. "Here."

"Boy, I know you didn't." She started.

"Get yo' thick ass in the car so we can holler." I said, stepping back into the street after letting two cars fly by on Michigan Avenue.

She closed the door. The seatbelt automatically came across her chest. "At least you noticed. And when you start talking to me any old kind of way, TJ? I thought you had more respect for me then that?"

I pulled off. "I thought you would have more respect for me than to be fucking my right-hand man. Since when you turned into a hoe?"

She gasped. "Really, boy? That's how we finna start this?"

"Bitch, you heard what I said. When you start fucking my nigga?" I got into traffic and started cruising with Moneybagg banging loud enough to make the trunk knock.

She sat there in silence. Then she cleared her throat again. "I never thought I would see the day that you disrespected me the way that you are doing. That shit making me wanna cry. Straight up."

I glanced at her from the corner of my eye. "Chill out with all that emotional shit, Jackie. Why you can't answer my question like a woman, huh? You acting like you're one of these young hoes I be fucking on."

"He was there, TJ. Damn, I just did a bid with you. You wasn't even out that long before you went right back. I bumped into Juelz a few times here and there. Then he asked me out to lunch. I got to seeing so many of your traits inside of him that it made me wet. You already know I got a thing for young men. Y'all do something to me. Especially the thugs. But long story short, we fucked around a few times, and that's just that."

I nodded. "Cool. I mean I ain't got no ring on yo' finger no way. You do what you wanna do."

"You damn right I do. Now why you ain't call me? You feeling some type of way because I fucked with him or something? That jail shit done made you turn into a bitch? Huh?" She asked looking like she was getting riled up.

I turned to her and laughed. "Shut yo' ass up. Ain't no ma'fuckin' hoes over here. I don't give a fuck if you screwing my nigga or not. I just gave you more credit than that, but you do you. Maybe one of these days we'll come through and flip yo' ass or something." I snickered at that.

"TJ, you testing my patience. Why are you coming at me so bogus? Did mama hurt your heart, baby?"

"Save that shit. That shit used to be special when I thought it was just our thing. Now that I clearly see you just like young niggas, and you play the mother role with all of them, man fuck that. We ain't on that." I rolled around the block and cruised down it. "I need some money. N'all, better yet, I need you to invest in me some property. I can't be in these streets forever, and I know you got plugs everywhere. What do you say about helping me get my foot into the real estate game?"

"After the way you been talking to me? Really?" She looked out of her passenger's window.

"Yo, you acting like one of them young hoes again. We on something else right now. Look at me when I'm talking to you, Jackie."

She turned to stare at me. "What do you want, TJ?" Her eyes looked down to the Tech on my lap.

I adjusted it. "I said I need you to help me get into the real estate market. I need some capital. I need some property. I need some of your influence."

"Boy, have you even went to school for real estate?" She asked, looking irritated.

"N'all, but I signed up for three classes online, and I gotta go to two physically. I start this fall."

"You fa real?" She looked excited.

"Yeah, I'm for real."

She leaned across the console and kissed my cheek. "I'm proud of you, baby. I swear I am. And you damn right I'll help you in the game. I been moving and grooving a lil' bit. I made some connections that'll get you right. Chicago been moving around a bunch of poor folk from the inner city so they can move their rich folk closer to down-town. That is leaving a lot of property available in the ghetto for whoever wants to buy it up. I been doing it be-cause I have insiders telling me that the state is about to buy them back from me at a higher rate so they can tear the houses down and rebuild as condominiums. I will be able to more than double my money a year from now."

"That sound good. I want in." I said looking over to her.

"What's in it for me?" She asked, placing a tuft of hair behind her right ear.

"What do you want?"

"That threesome that you spoke of. I wanna have both of my babies fucking me all weekend in every home that I got. I'm talking on some real freaky shit, too. Whatever I say goes."

"If you thinking about some fruity shit, that ain't hap-pening. I'll blast yo' ass, talking stupid like that, too."

"Fruity? Boy, n'all. I want y'all fucking me. Not no other weird shit. I can't believe that would even come out of your mouth."

"Well, it did. When you tryna get yo' ass flipped?" I asked cutting to the chase.

"Well, my birthday is in three weeks. How about I fly y'all out to Jamaica with me, and we can fuck like rabbits all weekend? I'll even take y'all shopping and allow for you to run up a check. Deal?"

"I gotta get Juelz on board, but I'm sho it ain't gon' be hard. We got a deal. Let me see something though."

"What?"

I pulled the car behind her G Wagon and took my seatbelt off. Then I leaned over into her. Yanked her skirt backward and stuck my hand between her thighs.

"Wait, TJ." She tried to grab my wrist.

I moved her lil' hand out of the way. Felt back between her thighs. Pulled her panties to the right, and tried to go into her hefty pussy lips, but was restricted from doing so.

"Boy, I was trying to tell yo' ass that it's that time of the month for me." She rolled her eyes.

I still felt around. I was trying to make sure that her pussy was still tight as it had always been, but the tampon stopped me from doing so. "This pussy still tight?" I asked taking my fingers from her middle and wiping them down with a wet wipe.

"Been tight all my life. It ain't gon' change either. I'm forty-six years old and still bleeding. That ought a tell you something."

"Yeah, it tell me that I can't bust in yo' ass or you might be in trouble. Get out my shit. Yo' number still the same right?"

"Did you just tell me to get out yo' shit like I'm a Peon or something?"

"Yep. Yo' number still the same?"

She nodded. "Yeah, it is." She lowered her head and pulled her skirt down. "You really hurting my feelings, TJ. I thought we were tighter than this. Why are you treating me like shit?"

I sighed. "Get out, Jackie. I got some shit to do. I'll fuck with you in a minute."

She took off her seatbelt and opened the door. "Okay, TJ. Well, I guess I'll see you later. I love you, boy."

"Yep. I'll be in touch." I leaned over and closed the door. Then drove off, leaving her at the curb looking stupid. I didn't give a fuck. Hearing that she was fucking with Juelz had crushed me. I honestly loved Jackie because she held me down during my worst time which was my first incarceration. I couldn't even look at her without reminiscing about all of the good times we'd had. I shook my head and had to remember that heartless niggas weren't painless.

***

"When we gon' start talking to each other again, Sodi?" I asked as we sat in the dark with candles on the table. I called myself trying to be all romantic. I surprised her with a T-Bone steak dinner with all of the fixings. Ran her bath water, and had rose petals all over the house, and it was like none of it meant anything to her.

She sat across from me picking at her food like she knew it was laced with cooties. "I don't know what there is to talk about, TJ. I guess I'm just depressed. I still ain't did my college homework. I got too much stuff on my mind." The candlelight glimmered off of her beautiful face. She was without makeup, but she was still cold. Her long, curly hair was all over her chest and back.

"Baby, why are you depressed? Is it because of something that I have done?" I asked her, knowing damn well that it had to be.

"I don't know. I think my thing is that I'm just starting to become so addicted to you that it's making me sick. My mother always said that my biggest curse would be that I would love my man too hard. Now I see what she means."

She sighed. "I know you're cheating on me, and I hate it. I wanna leave you, but I love you too much."

"Why do you think I'm cheating on you?"

"Nigga, a better question is why are you cheating on me? What am I doing wrong?" She looked over to me. Her eyes were glossy. I could tell that she was seconds away from crying. That affected me.

I looked off. "Baby, you're not doing anything wrong. I love you."

She shook her head. "No, you don't. Don't even say that shit to me. If you loved me, you would not be doing the things that you are. Love doesn't hurt this much." She closed her eyes. Tears fell down her cheeks. "All I can be is the best possible version of myself. I can give you all that I got, every single day, and that will be the best that I can do. I'm starting to see that it won't be enough for you though, now would it?"

Damn, she had me feeling like shit. I hated making a female cry that I cared about. I never wanted to hurt Sodi. She was a good girl. I really did love her, but that street shit was just in me way too tough. I wish it wasn't, but it was. "Baby. What can I do to show you that I love you, and that you matter to me? Name it and watch me do it."

She shook her head. "TJ, if you ain't doing it already, then I guess you never will. Besides, this is more my fault than it is yours. I thought I could change you. I thought that I could make you fall in love with me and then it would always be all about me. That's what's wrong with us women. We always feel like we can change a man until his true nature brings us to our reality. When a man is a dog, he's nine times out of ten staying a dog. It's unfortunate, but it's a fact." She dropped her fork and stood up.

"I appreciate the dinner, TJ. Have a good night. I need to be alone for a little while."

I sat there at the table for the next half hour stuck. I didn't know what to do. I wanted to go into the back room and console her. I wanted to let her know how much I loved her, but I didn't. I stayed put because I was unsure of myself and what it is that I really wanted in life. So, I gave her space and kept my distance, even though we stayed under the same roof.

T.J. Edwards

Chapter 15

A week later Punkin handed me a small white envelope and took a step back. We were outside of her two-story bricked home in Evanston. She had a certain pep to her step and seemed giddy. "TJ, I just want you to keep an open mind. Know that I love you, and I'm ready to be with you faithfully right now. Whatever decision you make, I'll be woman enough to accept it."

I frowned. Mugged her while I opened the letter. Inside of it was two little ultrasound pictures. I looked up to her. "What's this?"

She rubbed her stomach in a circle. "I'm pregnant, TJ, and you're going to be a daddy." She smiled and looked me over real carefully. "How do you feel?"

I kept looking over the shots. I could barely tell what was what, but I kept looking. "How far along are you?"

"About five weeks. Yep. I am so excited. You still didn't tell me how you're feeling."

"It's because I don't honestly know. I mean, I care about you. But I care about Sodi a lot too. This shit finna damage us."

She cringed. "What? Are you serious? That's your response. You're going to bring up your relationship with her while holding our child's ultrasound?" She snatched it from me. "How dare you?" She stormed into her house.

I stood in the sun with my hand over my forehead. I was sick. Not only because I didn't know if I was ready to be a father, but also because of my response to her. No female wanted the first words from a man when she'd given him this kind of news to have been what mine were. I felt stupid. I slowly made my way to her front door. I had to apologize, but when I tried the knob it was locked. I knocked on the door.

"Go away, TJ. I hate you!" She hollered.

I beat some more. "Pleases open up, Punkin. I'm sorry for what I said to you. You didn't deserve that."

"Well, you feel how you feel. It is what it is. I'll figure this out on my own anyway. I should have known that you were going to do me like this. I just gave you more of a benefit of than the doubt!" It sounded like she was crying.

Now I was really feeling like shit. I rang the doorbell and beat on the door again. "Baby, I'm sorry. I swear I want us to talk about this. You ain't finna do this shit on your own. That's for damn sure. Now come on. Shorty, open up." I waited impatiently. I could hear the birds chirping in the tree that were in her yard. I heard the locks click. Then it was silent. I turned the knob and stepped into her place.

The first thing I smelled was a Glade scented plug-in. It made the house smell fresh and welcoming. The inside was elegant. She had white leather furniture. The walls were white, yet the paintings hanging on them were outlined in black frames. From as far as I could see her entire home was made up in black and white. I nodded at her swag.

She was sitting on the sofa with the ultrasound pictures on the table. "I know that we're young, TJ, but I know that we can give this child a good life if we get our things in order right now. I've been kicking butt in college. I have more money than I can spend, and there appears to be more to come from my grandparents once they pass away. I mean, financially we're sound. All we have to do is get you in order. There is no way that I would ever want to raise a child on my own. I mean, as a woman I know that I am strong enough to do anything, but I just wouldn't want to. I feel that every child should have both parents in the household. That will give our child a double chance at surviving. What do you think?"

"Punkin, first of all, I just gotta ask. Are you absolutely sure that there is no other possibilities outside of me that could be the father?"

She nodded. "I cross my heart and hope to die. I have only been with one other man outside of you, and that was almost a year ago. He lives in Gary, Indiana."

I nodded. I kneeled beside her and rested my hand on her stomach. "I don't feel it kicking. What, is it sleep or something?"

She laughed. "Boy, it's only about five weeks. The damn baby probably ain't even got a heartbeat yet. But you're cute, you know that?"

I blushed as much as a dark brown colored man could. I was embarrassed. I should've known that information. "Yo, I ain't never did this before. This is all going to be new to me so you gon' have to stay on me. I wanna make sure that you have a good pregnancy. That way our child can come out all healthy and strong."

She smiled, then looked down on me. Her little hand rested on top of my dreads. "I don't wanna make things difficult for you. I know that we both have a bunch of growing up to do. We are just going to have to do it as fast as possible. We got nearly nine months to be in a better position. The streets have to be an afterthought. Our baby is going to need you." She rubbed the side of my face. "What are we going to do about Sodi? When she find out, I see that girl being ready to kill something."

I shrugged. "I need you to give me some time before I tell her. I can't just spring this shit on her. I done denied fuckin' with you on a few occasions. All it's gone take is for her to add up the dates, and then all hell gon' break loose. I need at least a month. Can you give me that?"

"Seeing as she most likely gon' come and kill me first because I done lied to her about having any interest in you as well, I think you should take two months. But sooner or later you are going to have to tell her. But then what?"

"What do you mean?"

She smacked her lips. "Boy, are we going to be together or not? I need to know ahead of time what I'm getting myself into."

I didn't know the answer to that either. I was only nineteen. Seeing myself locked down to one female for the rest of my life seemed nuts. There was way too much pussy out there. I mean, true enough, Punkin was probably the finest Black female I had seen in my entire life, but even still, there were too many other races of women that were in the world that I wanted to explore. Not to even mention that my thing for older women was serious. So, I didn't think I could submit to a life of one woman, at least not yet. But by the way Punkin was looking at me, I knew I couldn't tell her that. She looked too fragile. "The only way we are going to be able to raise up a strong child is if we are together, so you already know what it is."

Punkin jumped up, and screeched. I stood up. She wrapped her arms around my neck. "Oh, baby, I love you so, so much. I wasn't ready for this to happen, but now that it has, I'm glad that it happened with you." She kissed me and moaned into my mouth. "You're the best."

***

Four hours later I was rolling in the passenger seat of Juelz's new platinum Benz with a baby assault rifle on my lap. He looked over at me and frowned. "Dawg, you been quiet for a minute. I ain't never heard you this quiet. What's up?"

I shook my head. "Just thanking 'bout some shit. That's all."

"Something like what? I need you to tell me what's good before we get over here to these white hoes' condo. Bruh, you ain't finna be no party pooper. I need you to be on your game. It's these bitches last night in town before they fly back to Dubai. We gotta get it in."

"Punkin pregnant."

He snapped his neck to look over at me. "By you?"

I nodded. "Yep."

"Aw, shit nigga, I gotta find me a new right-hand man."

"Shut up, dawg."

"Sodi finna kill yo' ass, and Punkin. You know that. I keep telling you that Puerto Ricans are crazy, especially when they fall in love with a nigga. She ain't finna honor you and old girl having no kid together. Trust me when I tell you this. You finna murder one, or the both of y'all."

I mugged his dumb ass. "Dawg, you think I'm finna let a ma'fucka just kill me? You got me fucked up." I snapped.

He laughed. "You know what I mean, nigga. When you finna tell her?"

I shrugged. "I don't know. Probably in a week or so."

"Man, you need to keep this shit a secret as long as you can. At least until you can find a way to break it down to her. Right now, it's a disaster. That girl love you. You finna shatter her."

I lowered my head. "I know. I fucked up. But it's already in the making. Ain't nothing I can do about it."

Juelz shook his head. "Damn, but Punkin though? Nigga, you been loving her ass anyway. Ever since we was some little ass kids. Now you finna have a whole ass baby by her. That shit wild business." He looked over at me. "She got some bomb, don't she?"

"Nigga, what?" I was offended.

"Come on now, TJ, this is me. Nigga, we talk about everything. I just always wondered how she was in the sack. At least tell me that she got a nice lil' wet shot."

"Juelz, shorty having my seed done placed her on a whole other level. That's a jewel to me now. I ain't finna talk about what her pussy like, nigga. You shouldn't be worried about that shit no way."

"Oh, I gotta wonder. You see, because she having yo' seed, I will never try and fuck her bad ass. That's out of love for you. But it's good. If she got you defending her like this, then she gotta have some bomb ass pussy. That's common sense." He stepped on the gas.

"Bruh, hurry up and get us to these white bitches' crib so I can take my anger out on one of they lil' pink boxes. You starting to give me a headache."

He laughed. "N'all, yo' situation giving you a headache. You might have high blood pressure."

"N'all, nigga, I got you for a right hand. That's all it take."

"I love you too, shorty." He busted up laughing and sparked a Garcia Vega blunt stuffed with that yellow OG Lemon Kush.

***

I sat back on the couch an hour later while Juelz dumped some pink ninety percent pure cocaine out on the table and got to separating it into twelve lines. He looked up. "Yo, this shit here straight from Columbia. It's about to have yo' model bitches acting all kinds of crazy." They laughed at his remark and kept sipping their Patron while Cardi B banged out of the speakers.

I had Sodi on my mind real tough. I was expecting for her to hit me, but as I looked at the face of my phone I saw that she hadn't called me even once. I sent her a quick text letting her know that I loved her and hit her ass with a few lovey-dovey emojis.

One of the white girls from my birthday party slid on the couch next to me. She took a baby sip from her champagne glass and smiled. She was the one that had the dark black hair and blue eyes. Out of the three from my party she had the best body and was the most gorgeous to me.

"You're TJ, right?"

I nodded. "The one and only."

"Right. Didn't we get sort of get acquainted at your party a few weeks ago?" Her breath smelled of the Patron and mint.

I looked her over. She had on a short black mini skirt that was half up her thighs. She opened them slightly, and I saw a hint of her white panties. Her breasts were spilling out of the white beater that she wore without a bra. "Yeah, but today is a new day. What's really good?"

She grinned and took another sip of the Patron. She sat the glass on the tables and sunk to her knees. "I've never in my life been with a Black dude before. If my parents even knew that I was considering it, they would cut me off faster than Donald Trump did Rudy Giuliani." She rubbed over my lap. "Can I see it?"

"Gone 'head."

She unzipped me quick and pulled my piece out. Her eyes got as big as plates. She licked her lips. "Damn, now this is a cock. I'm with you for the night. You hear me?" She licked her lips again and started stroking me.

"Cool."

Her mouth covered him. Then she was sucking like she had something to prove, while she rubbed my stomach. Her lips were tight and wet. Her head game was on point.

I pulled down the straps of her beater. Her plump, tanned titties popped out. They knocked into each other while she bobbed her head in my lap, breathing hard.

"I want his cock so bad," she said, popping me out. Then she was sucking again at full speed. Her hand went between her thighs. She moaned. Took her head away, and played between her thighs for a second, then grabbed my piece again, and got to sucking.

I laid all the way back. I saw how her long hair was all over the place, and I made my mind up, I was finna fuck this lil' bitch. "Yo, Juelz, toss me a rubber!" I hollered.

He already had one of the snow bunnies bent over the table, fucking her at full speed. He stopped and threw me a roll of Magnums.

I pushed her off of me and handed it to her. "Put this ma'fucka on with yo' mouth."

She squeezed her titties together. The pink tips were well distended. "Yes, baby." She opened the package and

144

put the plastic into her mouth with ease. Then she was applying the rubber to my dick slowly.

I reached across her back and squeezed that ass. It wasn't as big as what I was used to, but I was finna beat that shit in regardless. When I took my fingers away from her skin, the prints of them were still there until it faded away a few seconds later.

"How do you want me? Tell me? Please." She stood up and rubbed her box. It was cleanly shaven. Looked plump, and engorged.

I stood up and flung her over the arm of the sofa. Grabbed her small hips and smacked her on that ass hard.

She yelped. "Awww! Fuck yeah! Harder." She hissed.

"What would yo' daddy say, bitch, if he knew I was finna put all this black meat in yo' ass? Huh?" *Smack!* I hit her ass so hard that my hand got to stinging.

She started shaking and bucked. A thick trail of juice came out of her pussy. "Fuck me! Fuck me, please, or kill me."

I got behind her ass and slid in hard. As soon as I shot through those sex lips, I started to try and kill her. I was banging that pink pussy hard.

Bam! Bam! Bam! Bam!

She threw her head back and screamed while she rocked. Her big titties danced on her chest. "Aww. Aww. Yes. Yes. He's so deep. He's so deep. Awww, fuck meeee-a!" She screamed. Then came with her face in the couch.

I started smacking that ass again. It was beet red already. The redder it got, the more I beat it. Fucking her harder and harder.

Juelz was banging one of the girls while the bitch he was banging had her face in the other redhead's pussy, eating her hungrily. I looked back down at my Snow Bunny. I watched how it looked for my dark piece to go in and out of her pink box. She kept getting wetter and wetter. Coming back to back.

I pulled out and folded her lil' ass up, banging as hard as I could while her hard nipples poked against my lips, begging me to suck them until I did. I pulled them with my teeth while my hips continued to slam into her, faster and faster. She was screaming. I sucked her nipple, and ran my tongue in circles around it, until I came, jerking into her pussy. As soon as I stood up and pulled the rubber off, I stroked him, cumming all over her chest and neck. She pulled my piece to her and sucked me dry. Then begged for me to fuck her again. Me and Juelz didn't leave their pad until early the next morning.

Chapter 16

When I got home the next morning, Sodi was in the middle of the living room floor with her head down. I could tell that she had been crying because there were Kleenexes all over the carpet. I rushed to her side and fell to my knees. "Baby, what's the matter? Why didn't you answer my texts?"

"They killed him, TJ. They murdered him right in front of my mother's porch." She jumped up and rushed into my arms. Crying hard. She wrapped her little arms around my neck and squeezed me tight. I didn't even know who she was talking about, but I felt bad for her. She held me for a second, then she pushed me away. "Where were you when I needed you last night?" She snapped.

I felt terrible. "What are you talking about? I texted you. You the one didn't get back to me. I ain't do nothing wrong." These were the words coming out of my mouth, and as I heard them, I nearly wanted to apologize.

She mugged me with seething anger. "Twenty times, muthafucka. I messaged you back twenty times last night after you hit me up once. You didn't respond. You didn't even read my fuckin' messages. I been in this house sick after leaving my mother at the fuckin' morgue. Do you have any idea how much I needed you last night?" She cried, with snot coming out of her nose.

I stepped forward and held out my arms. "Baby, please come here." I stepped toward her.

She took three steps back. "N'all, fuck that, TJ. I'm hurting right now. I deserve better than this." She sat on the sofa and dropped her head. Her long, curly hair dragged against the carpet.

I came over and kneeled beside her. "Baby, who was it? Who got killed?"

She lifted her head and glared at me. She tried to maintain her mug, but her weakness set in. She melted. She sunk to the floor on her knees. "They killed Roberto. My older brother. He was all that I had in this world outside of my mother. Now he's gone. What am I going to do? TJ, please tell me." She wailed and fell against me.

I held her in my arms as tight as I could without hurting her. I felt sick. I literally felt like I had the flu. I couldn't believe that my woman was going through all of this while I was laid up with a bunch of nobody ass bitches. I felt like kicking my own ass. She was right. She did deserve more than what I was giving her. She had lost a whole ass brother while I was pounding out a Snow Bunny. Damn, I was bogus.

Sodi sniffled and came to her feet. "They tried to rob him. They shot him seven times, and he held on all the way until I got to him. Then he passed away in my arms." She shook her head. "I swear to God that life sucks." She cried.

"Baby, I'm sorry that this happened, but I need you to know that I love you. I love you with all of my heart, and I promise to stand by your side through all of this."

She wiped away her tears. "I'm still mad at you, but I do need you. I'm hurting so bad." She cried.

***

We had Roberto's funeral five days later on the Westside of Chicago, at a church on Beecher and Spaulding, right in the heart of Humboldt Park. I was there to support Sodi, but man I did not like being in that area at all. Roberto was a high-ranking gang member. He had all kinds of coldblooded killers that filled the church of his funeral service. The colors were gold and black. The only exception was for their mother Lucy. She was allowed to wear an all-black gown with a veil over her face. I was told the dress code ahead of time, so I fell in line. In Chicago, if you wanted to stay alive you fell in line and followed the protocol of whatever hood you were in. If a ma'fucka told you to take your hat off for whatever reason, you took it off, and you kept it off, or you lost your life. If they told you the colors were gold and black, and you ignored it, nine times out of ten your funeral would be the next one that was being held. I wasn't with all that shit, so I got fitted in an all-black Roberto Cavalli suit with the gold button up underneath. Even the handkerchief in my suit pocket was gold. I blended in.

Sodi came and grabbed my hand mid-way through the service. She took me up to the front so I could look down on her brother. I took a deep breath and looked him over. He was laid inside of a gold coffin. The interior was all black. They suited him in a black and gold Armani suit. There were staples in his forehead from where I guessed the bullets had did their damage. The mortician did his best to piece him back together. He looked very pale, and small. I had never met him before, but I guess I always imagined him being so much bigger because he is Sodi's or was Sodi's big brother. But he looked like a little guy.

I shook my head. "I'm so sorry, Mami."

"He loved me, TJ. He really did. He was the only one that I knew would protect me against all odds. Now he's gone. What am I going to do?"

I squeezed her hand. "You got me. I'm here for you, and I ain't going no muthafuckin' where."

She shushed me. "Hey, watch your mouth." She did the sign of the crucifix over her body. "We're in a church, Daddy."

One of Roberto's killers stepped to the side of me. "Say, Homes, no disrespect, but there is a lot of the Vatos that want to give Roberto their last respects, so if you two don't mind?" He opened his hand, leading us away from the coffin.

Sodi flared her nostrils. "Emilio, I know you're not up here trying to rush me the way that I think you're doing." She snapped. "My brother never got a chance to meet my man, so I'm introducing him right now. If you got a problem with that then I don't know what the fuck to tell you." Her face began to turn red.

Emilio was a heavy-set, Mexican nigga, with a bunch of tattoos all over his face. He had a gold crown right under his left eye, and two tear drops under his right. "Lo siento, Sodi? Take as much time as you need. I didn't mean to offend you." He bowed his head and backed away from us.

Sodi grabbed my hand and brought me closer. She took a deep breath. "Forgive me for my language, Santa Maria." She ran her fingers through her hair. "Okay. TJ, this is Roberto. Roberto, this is my man. His name is Thylonius, but everybody calls him TJ. I'm sorry that I never got around to introducing you two when you were alive, but I'm doing it now." Tears ran down her cheeks some more. She pulled her Chanel sunglasses off of the V neck of her dress and placed them on her face. She sniffled.

"TJ. Baby. Is there anything that you would like to say to Roberto?"

I was weirded out by what Sodi was doing, but I knew that she was just trying her best to heal, so I went along with it. "Yo, Roberto. I'm sorry that we had to meet on these terms. I hear that you were a real good dude. You sister really loved you, and I love her. I promise to take care of her for you. I'ma hold her down, and make sure that your mother stay straight. You got my word on that."

Sodi leaned into the casket and kissed his cheek. "I love you, big bruh. Be cool up there. Make sure you give Santa Maria all the respect that she deserves. Please." She kissed him again and backed away from the casket. "Come on, baby. Now we can let these other people say their goodbyes."

***

It started to pour down raining as soon as we got to the cemetery. There was no thunder and lightning, but it looked like a tropical storm was brewing. Sodi said a prayer over Roberto's graves before she got down on one knee chanting while they lowered him into the ground. Her mother stood behind us crying. Emilio consoled her. I felt sick and imagined what she must have been feeling. I didn't know what to say to her, but I felt I should've said something.

I waited until Sodi got up. I dusted her off as best I could. She leaned against me for support while we headed back over to where her mother was. When we got in front of her, thunder roared overhead for the first time, and it became dark inside of the cemetery.

Sodi looked up to me. "Baby, just go over there and give my mother a hug. She'll be tense at first but then she'll melt."

I nodded and released my hold on her. I walked beside Emilio. "Say, bruh, I just wanna hug Ms. Jimenez."

He nodded. "Okay."

I stepped in front of her and pulled her respectfully into my arms. Once there, I held her, and kissed her cheek. She'd done exactly what Sodi said. At first, she seemed tense, then she melted once my arms were all the way around her. "I'm sorry for your loss, Ms. Jimenez. If there is anything that you need, please don't hesitate to let me know."

She nodded. "Gracias, mijo." Which meant *thank you my son*.

Sodi grabbed my hand, and after she hugged her mother again, we jogged to my car, and got in. I drove away with my heart heavy for her. I didn't know for sure what she was going through, but I knew that she was hurting. I was willing to do anything to take that hurt away from her.

She sat in the passenger seat quiet. Tears continued to pore. "TJ, I swear to God I feel like dying right now." She sniffled. "I don't think I can take this pain." Her voice began to crack up.

"Don't say that, Sodi. I would lose my mind if something happened to you. I love you too much to even imagine some shit like that."

"My brother and I had been through so much together. We literally have eaten off of the floor to survive. Life for us sucked but we got through it together. He always told me how special I was. I'm really gone miss him."

I reached over and wiped her tears. "I got you though, boo. Anything you need, I'ma be right here for you."

"Thank you, I appreciate that." She was quiet for a few moments. Then she adjusted in her seat. "When we get home, there is something that I gotta show you because I don't know what to do with it. Okay?"

I nodded. "Yeah, baby. Don't you want us to hit up the repass first?"

She thought about it for a minute, then shook her head. "N'all. I ain't got no appetite for food. I just want to get home and cuddle until I can close my eyes. I feel like I ain't got a good night's sleep since two days before I even found out that this had happened to him." She turned to me. "Can you hold me all night long?"

"You know I will. I'll do whatever it takes to make you happy."

***

When we got home, instead of Sodi showing me what she needed to, she stripped at the front door. Then she took me out of my wet clothes, and we left them in a pile right in the vestibule of her house. She held my hand until we got in the bedroom. Once there, she had me lay on my back, then she climbed on top of me, and hugged me tight. "I just want you to hold me until the pain stops, TJ. I can't take what I'm feeling. Why does life have to hurt so bad?" She cried. Her tears ran down the side of my neck.

I held her and rubbed her back. "I got you, boo, and I ain't going nowhere." I held her for the rest of that night, and for two days straight after that. I would have held her for an entire week if she needed me to.

Chapter 17

"Nigga, I know you remember that fool Blue from Punkin party back in the day. You remember, the one you had to rough up from trying to take the pussy from yo' baby mama?" Juelz said before turning up his pink Sprite.

I sat in the driver's seat looking over at him. It was a full week later, and we were supposed to be getting on a plane later that day so we could fly down to Jamaica and handle Jackie on that freaky shit. She had already booked the first-class roundtrip flights.

"Yeah, what about him?" I asked growing a lil' impatient. Sodi was getting better but I could tell that she still needing my constant presence. Punkin was blowing up my phone like crazy too, but since things had taken place with Sodi's brother, I had been blowing her off more than I should have. I had too much shit going on, and I didn't know what to do.

"Turns out that he linked up with your brother Deion. Deion had given him the order to gun our ass down on the night that we got shot up. Your brother also paid that nigga seventy-five gees up front for him to capture you and bring you to him."

"How you find all of this out?"

"His baby mama was in the next room on the night that Deion and Blue made this deal. The old one, and this new one. He got most of his niggas from No Love City looking for you and me. That's new to me, but this bitch ain't got no reason to lie."

"Why the fuck would she be telling you all of this? Especially if Blue is her baby daddy?"

"She just found out that she pregnant with my shorty too. She three months. Her and that nigga ain't laid down since before their three-year-old was born."

I looked him over from the corners of my eye. "Bruh, what type of shit you on?"

"Nigga, let me finish. That ain't even the kicker. Blue just came up on the Jay's list."

"The Jay's list? What the fuck is that?"

"He's in knee-deep debt with the Cartel. It's fifty bands on his head. Him and his brother Packee. The kicker also is that they finna be right where we're going to vacation."

"In Jamaica?"

"Bingo." Juelz said. "So, why we finna use this bitch to get us down there, we gon' make fifty bands along the way. How that sound?"

I didn't know how I felt about that. I didn't want to leave Sodi. Even though she was giving me her blessing to go and handle my business, business that she thought included the game, I still felt like it was too premature to be leaving her on her own. I just didn't feel right about it. "Bruh, my lady still going through some thangs. I don't even know if I could make Jamaica."

"What? Didn't you hear me say you can make fifty gees?"

"I heard you. But you ain't been with her while she been going through this shit. She is the weakest that I have ever seen her."

"But I thought you told me that you hollered at her already?" Juelz said, looking irritated.

"I did, but still in all, I can tell when something ain't right. And I'm telling you that she still weak."

He shook his head in disgust. "I mean, I understand that she been through the ringer for the last few weeks, but this is fifty gees. I can't see how you finna past this up." He took three pulls off of his blunt and inhaled the smoke. Then blew it towards the ceiling of the whip. "Then, shorty saying that she already booked the flights. She got us our passports and shit. You finna break up all that shit just because your woman going through something that is a natural part of life? That's crazy, bruh, even for you." He let his seat all the way back and acted like he was in his feelings.

All I kept thinking about was the fact that I still had to tell Sodi about Punkin being pregnant with my seed. I already knew that when that finally came out that it was going to be severely damaging to our relationship. I didn't want to hurt her more than I already had.

"Bruh, I'll tell you what. If you come, nigga, you can keep the whole fifty bands. And, plus, I got another move lined up down there that will spring about that same amount of cash. I'll split that bitch with you down the middle. So, now you go from only having twenty-five thousand to seventy-five gees. You can't beat that. Even if she's going through something right now, when you come back you can buy her a nice present. All women love presents, especially when it's jewelry." He started to toke from his cigar of bud again.

Now my eyes were big. I was trying to see things through the windows of Sodi's eyes and emotions, and no matter how much I tried, I just kept seeing that there was seventy-five thousand dollars on the table to be made. That money was enticing. "Yo, I'll tell you what. Let me holler at her one more time tonight. I just wanna feel her out to make sure that she is good. After I let her know what kind of cash I'ma be bringing in, her reaction gon' tell me everything."

"Man, fuck that reaction. Nigga, come get this paper. Shorty is Puerto Rican. She is a fighter. She will be okay. Trust me on that. You need to fly down here. Flip this bitch with me. Hit her pockets for these properties. Then hit these other licks with me down there and come back with your bag all the way up. Once you got that cash in hand, you'll be able to deal with whatever you gotta deal with back here, including that beef shit with Deion. I hope you know that it's only a matter of time before he mount up and come for you. And if we don't go down here and snuff this nigga Blue, him and his crew coming for us too. So, you really gotta ask yourself how much is a bitch's emotions really worth when we got all of this shit on the line?"

I sat there lost in deep thought. Juelz was laying it on real thick. I didn't appreciate him calling Sodi a bitch, but then again I knew it was just his way. Second to that thought, he really had a point. If Deion was outsourcing the hit on my life into other crews, and Blue's was the first to get the job, then I needed to annihilate him to set a precedent. Then once my paper was right from the job of knocking his head loose, I had to go at Deion and get rid of his bitch ass. If I didn't, I was certain that he would come for me when I least expected it.

"Nigga, I know you better than anybody else on this earth. Right now, all of that shit going through your head. You starting to see it real clearly. You already know we gotta handle this business, don't you?"

As fucked up as it was, he was right. "Yeah. I'm still finna get shit right with her. Then I'll meet up with you tomorrow afternoon so we can get on that flight together. Cool?"

Juelz nodded with a big ass smile on his face. "Cool, nigga. Jamaica, here we come."

***

When I made it back to Sodi's place that night, Punkin was sitting across the street in her black Benz. She flashed her bright lights three times to get my attention. When I looked across the street, she rolled down her tinted windows and waved me over.

I looked up at the house I should've been walking into, and reluctantly came across the street. She popped the door to her passenger's side. I got in. "Girl, what yo' ass doing over here? You hollered at Sodi or somethin'?" I gave her a suspicious look.

"N'all, I ain't talked to her. Damn. And that's what you say to me after avoiding me for the last few days? What's your problem?"

I pointed. "Shorty, roll off. I ain't got no problem."

She started the car and pulled away from the curb. "Why have you been avoiding me? Are you trying to tell me something?" She asked looking over to me.

"N'all, I ain't trying to tell you nothing. I just been going through a lot with her ever since she lost her brother. That's why I ain't had the chance to get up with you. I know you can understand that."

"I can. I mean, to a certain degree. I still feel like you should've been man enough to tell me that. Things haven't been the greatest for me either. I've been very sick and

159

throwing up so much that I had to drive myself to the hospital the other night. They told me that I needed to stay in a state of rest for a few days. I can't though. All I keep thinking about is you. I missed you, baby." She reached over and took a hold of my hand.

I allowed for her to hold it for a second, then moved it away from her. "Punkin, I don't know what I wanna do with all of this no more."

She withdrew her hand and kept rolling for a few streets. Then she sighed and looked over at me. "What are you taking about, TJ?"

"I'm talking about with everything. I feel like I been shitting on Sodi when she ain't been nothing but a good girl to me ever since we got together. I mean, she was the only one that held me down while I was on lock. That say a lot about a woman. I gotta be man enough to step up to the plate for her."

Punkin flared her nostrils. "So, because she held you down for eight months, you feeling like that gives you motive to be able to crap on me and this child I have brewing inside of me? Is that what you are saying?"

I shook my head. "Never. I would never leave any woman that had my seed out in the cold to fend for herself. I'm not saying that."

"Then what are you saying?"

"If you shut the fuck up so I can get my thoughts out then you'll be able to see where I'm coming from. Damn."

She balled her face. "You always tryna snap on somebody. Where is the love? Where is the respect for the woman that is about to bring you new life? I have never disrespected you. I have never done anything to you that would make you feel less than a man. Yet here you are making me chase your ass down because I'm so worried about you. Dizzy, and sick, but still on your fuckin' heels because I love you, and you got the nerves to tell me to shut the fuck up. Wow." She pulled the car to the side of the road. Cut the engine, and just sat there. "I'm listening. N'all, screw that. No, I'm not. TJ, are you about to shit on me?"

I shook my head. "I'm confused. I love Sodi. I really do. I know that she is probably who I am supposed to be with, yet I care about you too. You're about to have my child, and as a man it's only right that I figure things out with you. But how do I do that, and remain loyal to her as well?"

Punkin shrugged. "I don't know, but I don't want to be a part of this equation any longer."

"What are you talking about?"

"TJ, you keep saying how much you love that girl. You say that first. You don't refer to me, or our situation, until you make it perfectly clear that you care for her. That tells me everything that I need to know." She exhaled loudly. "I love you, but I'm not going to play second fiddle to no other female. I just can't. I need you to get out of my car. I'll figure things out on my own."

I mugged her. "Punkin, stop talking stupid. You are having our child. I'm not about to crap on you. I wanna be a part of its life. I wanna be a part of yours as well."

"N'all, TJ, I ain't looking for no baby daddy, baby mama type of relationship. I need a husband, and consistent father for the child that I am having. If I cannot have those things, then I prefer to be alone. It's no biggie! It's better than being hurt or worrying about where you are every second of the day. So, I'm going to drop you off on the corner of you and Sodi's street, and I'm going to go about my business." She started the car and pulled off.

"Punkin, I don't give a fuck what you are talking about out of anger. I'm going to be there for you and our baby. I just need a little time to get everything situated. Is that so much to ask?"

She shook her head. "Not anymore it isn't." She pulled to the corner of our street and stopped. "I love you, TJ. I wish you the best. I really mean that."

I stared at her for a long time. "Regardless to what you may believe, I love you, Punkin. I been in love with yo' ass since we were in kindergarten. I'ma get my stuff together, and I'm coming for you way before our child is born. I promise."

"Promises can only be proved with actions, never words. And if you can't hold me down throughout the entire pregnancy, then you don't deserve to be a part of me and this child's life. I'm sorry. I'll give you a few weeks to get yourself together. If there is no change by then, just forget about me."

***

When I made it into the house, Sodi was packing my suitcase. She had it laid on top of the bed. "Hey, Papi, how was your day?"

I grabbed her to me and held her for dear life. "I love you, Mami. I gotta get better at caring for you. I swear I do. I got one more thing I gotta do, then it's me and you, baby, from here on out; do you hear me?"

Her eyes were bucked. "Okay. Where is all of this coming from?"

"Just hear me out, okay?" I kissed her lips and held her for what seemed like an eternity. She felt so good in my arms. Her long hair fell over my arms and warmed me. The curls were so thick and rich.

"Daddy, I don't know what's going on inside of you, but I'm here if you wanna talk about it."

"N'all. Boo, I know what I gotta do, and I'm just finna do it and get it over with. But I swear to you when I get back, you and I are going to take our relationship to the next level. I promise you that."

She smiled. "Well that sounds good to me. I love you, Daddy."

"I love you too, baby."

T.J. Edwards

Chapter 18

I pushed the Chanel sunglasses up on my nose to block out the brightness of the Jamaican sun as I stepped off of the plane. There was a slight breeze. It smelled like ocean water. My clothes waved like a flag as I pulled my suitcase out of the airport, and to the curb.

Juelz lowered his Tom Ford sunglasses and peeped two thick ass Jamaican females as they walked past us with their asses shaking like a ma'fucka. Both were high yellow with long ass braids. He shook his head. "Nigga, I swear to God we hitting up the beach. I gotta see what all ass this ma'fucka got to offer." He said, still peeping the girls.

I laughed. "Shorty n'em thick as a muthafucka." I had to admit. I said it loud enough for them to hear me. They stopped and looked like they wanted to come back to see what was good. I threw my arms up. The sunlight shined off of my two chains. The diamonds in my TJ piece sparkled like a kaleidoscope.

Before they could make it back to us, Jackie blocked their path, and got wagging her finger. "Unn. Unn, lil' girls. Y'all gon' 'bout ya' business. These boys already spoken for." She told them.

"What?" Juelz stepped around her. "Yo, she tripping. What's good? Me and my brother tryna see what it do?" He jacked. His gold chains were shining just as hard. He had a piece that was of the Puerto Rican flag. It glistened in the light.

"Juelz, stop playing with me. Y'all ain't down here for them lil' hoes. Ya' hear for me. Now let's go." She chastised him.

I was already Facebooking Sodi. I was telling her how much I loved and missed her. She had already told me that while I was away that it was all she wanted to hear from me until I got back. She had plans on spending some time with her mother and siblings which I thought was cool. I honestly did miss her. At the same time, I couldn't get Punkin out of my brain either.

Jackie snatched my cellphone out of my hand all rude and shit. "Gimme this."

"Bitch." I grabbed my shit back. "Don't be snatching shit out of my hand. You got me fucked up." I took a step toward her.

She backed up. "Calm down, TJ. All I'm asking is that y'all give me my due while we're here. If y'all wanna be on your phones, and fuck off with some of the locals, that's fine, but just don't let me see it. I'm paying all of this money because I wanna have a good time with the both of y'all, and I want it to be special for me. Got it?"

"Yeah, I do, but if you snatch anything out of my hands again, you gon' be floating in that ma'fuckin' ocean. That's my word." I meant that shit too.

Juelz laughed, and slid his arm around her neck. "Baby, it's good. We finna treat this body right. You got us. Don't even trip, but you ain't gotta be all overbearing either. That ain't cool." He kissed her cheek.

She looked up at him. "Well, there are a bunch of beautiful young women down here. I can't help but to feel insecure. Y'all gon' have to help me with that along the way." She said this last part looking directly at me. "What's the matter with you, TJ?"

"Nothing. Come on. Let's get this show on the road."
I said, stepping up to the Navigator limousine as it pulled
up to the curb.

Two Jamaican handlers got out to assist us with our
bags. I saw that Jackie went all out for this trip. I guessed
a certain part of me felt that it was only right that me and
Juelz gave her exactly what she was paying for.

Juelz helped her inside of the truck. Then once all of
us were in and situated, he popped a bottle of Moët, and
poured her a glass. "Here you go, ma. I want you to have
the first glass because you are the most special person here
right now." He winked at me.

"Awww-uh, thank you, baby. I needed to hear that."
She kissed his lips and snuggled against him. After a few
seconds she patted the seat next to her. "Come here, TJ."

I turned off my phone and got up, sitting beside her.
Once there I went into mission mode. I rested my hand on
her right thick thigh and caressed it. "You been missing
yo' baby?"

She bit into her bottom lip. "Yeah. A whole, whole
lot."

I slid my hand under her shirt. Her chocolate thighs
were real thick, and healthy. I had to admit for an older
woman Jackie kept her body right. While I rubbed her
thigh, I took the time to squeeze it just to feel the firmness
of each one. She moaned and opened her thighs wider.
Now I was rubbing over her the front of her panties. The
lips felt meaty.

Juelz slid his hand into her top. He pulled out her right
breast, and flicked his tongue over her nipple, before he
sucked on it has if he was trying to get some milk out of
her. "You like that, baby, huh?"

"Yes. Mmm-hmm." She opened her thighs even wider.

I slid two fingers into her box, and casually ran them in and out. She was wet. Dripping her juices. My thumb would stop and rotate circles all over her clitoris that was standing up like a pinky finger.

"Go down on me, TJ. Please, baby. I need you to taste this pussy. I miss the way you do it." She moaned, as Juelz pulled out both of her breasts, and squeezed them together.

I slid to the carpeted limousine floor onto knees. Cocked her thighs wide open for old time sake and planted soft kisses on each thigh. She moaned and arched her back. My soft kisses turned into bites. Every time I rose from one place, I saw that I left a wet mark behind, then I was assaulting the next spot. My fingers dipped into her pussy deeper and deeper.

"Eat me, baby. Please. Unn. I can take this shit. I need to feel your mouth on my pussy. Y'all my boys." She placed her right foot up on the seat, busting her cat wide open. Her sex lips were dark chocolate. Her insides were bubblegum pink like a rare steak once you cut into it.

I blew on her pearl and kissed it. She shivered. My tongue lashed out and flicked it ten quick times. Then I slurped it into my mouth as if it were an oyster.

Jackie placed her thighs on my shoulders and pulled me to her in a death clutch. She rode my face hard, until she came, screaming at the top of her lings how much she missed me. I couldn't breathe. I just kept my tongue out and dug my nails into her legs. When she finally opened them, I was still licking and sucking like I was hungry. She had been the first woman to have taught me how to eat pussy, and now here she was reaping the benefits. Her pussy juice slid down my chin, and onto my neck.

Juelz pulled out his piece and grabbed a handful of her hair. "Come on, bitch. You already know what yo' baby want."

She licked her lips and sucked him into her mouth. The next thing I knew, she was sucking him fast-paced, slurping, and making a whole bunch of noise.

I leaned her on her side and raised her thigh into my right forearm. My rubber was already in place. With one forward motion of my hips, I slid into her, and yanked that ass back to me by use of her hips. Found my rhythm and got to fucking her for all she was worth; dipping into her tight box. She used her inner muscles on me almost immediately. Showing me what that vet shit was all about.

Juelz's eyes rolled into the back of his head. He jumped into her mouth again and again. "Her head game. Uh. Uh. Shit. This bitch." He kept humping. His eyelids closed tighter.

Jackie kept bobbing. She pulled her mouth from his piece and screamed as she felt me cumming hard. Her pussy muscles had worked me over. She pumped Juelz's pipe until he started to bust. It spit up onto her face, before she sucked him back into her mouth hungrily. He jerked and tried to push her off of him, but she had him in a death clutch it seemed.

I pulled out and took the rubber off. My dick kept jumping. The sight of her chocolate titties with the Hershey Kiss nipples were hot to me. I stroked my pipe for a few moments, looking at her chest.

After twenty minutes of us getting warmed up, the limousine pulled into the Paradise Island Resort that we were to be staying at. The handlers got out of the limo and knocked on the back doors. We were all just getting dressed. I was sure they smelled a wave of sex as soon as the doors were opened.

I climbed out and headed inside. Turned my phone back on and called Sodi. It may sound crazy, but I just wanted to hear her voice. I was missing her for some reason. Her phone kept ringing and ringing, and then it went straight to voicemail. That worried me, but I tried my best to not panic.

***

As soon as we got into the presidential suite, Jackie stopped in the middle of the floor, and dropped her clothes. "What do you say you come and take a shower with me, TJ, while Juelz roll us up a couple blunts?" She walked up to me and stopped in my face.

"That sound like a plan. Come on."

She took off walking in front of me. Her ass jiggling the whole way. She was a bad older bitch. Fine and chocolate. All it took was for me to tune into her body parts and I found myself lost all over again. That was that vet magic. I felt like only a sexy ass older woman could place that kind of spell over me.

She turned on the shower, and got the temperatures set just right while I got undressed and rubbed all over that big ass of hers. By the time we stepped inside, I was rock hard. I pushed her up against the wall. She placed her foot on the rim of the tub. I slid the Magnum down and dove into that pussy with a vengeance. Damn near picking her up with each thrust. I got to digging deep. She moaned with her face in the crux of my neck.

"Mmm. Mmm. Mmm. Fuck me, baby. Fuck me. Yes. Aww, shit I missed you. Awww. Awww. Shit."

I grabbed her thigh tighter and kept piping with my knees bent. "Shit, ma. Shit. This vet pussy. This that vet pussy."

She jumped and wrapped both of her thighs around me. I had to catch my balance, and crash into the tiled wall with her. Once there, I bounced her, giving her all of me. "Yes! Yes. Awww! Baby! This dick! Ooo, shit!" She licked along my neck and sucked on the thick vein there. I felt that pussy shaking as she came, screaming at the top of her lungs.

I busted again and pulled out. "Bitch, bend yo' ass over this ma'fuckin' tub. Hurry up!"

She made the transition on wobbly legs. She bent over and looked back at me. That chocolate ass was round. There were a few stretch marks across it that made it look super sexy too. Her pussy looked like it was breathing. The lips were slightly open. I rubbed into them and pinched her clit. She shrieked. "Fuck me, baby. I need you. Fuck me as hard as you can. Punish me."

I leaned down and kissed her right on both cheeks. They were hot. Then I got to rubbing all over them before my hand rose high. I brought it back down fast and hard. *Smack!*

She nearly stood up. "Uhhhh! Baby!"

Smack! I rubbed all over that ass again, and then dipped down and played with that leaking pussy. It dribbled all down her inner thighs. "You like that, ma? Huh?"

She looked over her shoulder at me with her eyes full of lust. Her tongue traced a circle around her lips. "It's time, lil' daddy. Fuck me, baby. Make me scream out. Please."

I grabbed her hips aggressively, and slammed home. My nails dug into her flesh while I pounded her strapped ass as hard as I could, watching my shit go in and out of her.

"Oh. Oh. Oh. Shit. Lil' daddy. My baby. Awww. Noooo. Shit, it hurt. Mmm. Baby. Baby." She arched her back again, and thaw her head back, screaming at the top of her lungs. Then she was cumming all over me.

Juelz stepped into the bathroom, smoking on a blunt. "Damn. Shorty, it sound like you in this ma'fucka killing her ass." He blew his smoke to the ceiling. "Switch, my nigga. You take the weed, and I'ma take mama."

She shivered at hearing him refer her as that. My dick slipped out of her, and rested against her ass, still rock hard. I circled her asshole with my middle finger. "Juelz, you ever hit this ass back here? Seeing as you done did everything else to my vet bitch?"

He shook his head. "N'all, not yet. But shorty 'bout ready to give her baby some of that back doe, ain't you, mama?"

I grabbed her by the hair and yanked her head backward. "Bitch, I wish you would say yeah. You already know who this shit belong to. Don't you?"

"Yes, baby." She looked so vulnerable.

I bent down and opened them chocolate ass cheeks. Her rosebud winked at me. Before I could even think about it, my lips were covering her asshole, and my tongue was shooting in and out of her. I was slobbering on purpose. Once I got it nice and wet, I got to easing into her. Pulling back on her hair.

She shuddered with every inch that I drove into her. "Lil' daddy. Ooo. You so big. It's too big."

I rubbed her pussy juices around the entrance before I slammed home. She hollered again. I didn't give a fuck. That back doe was super tight, and hot. It got me to shaking while I smacked those cheeks and fucked her like it was new pussy.

She bounced back into me. She kept looking over her shoulders at me. "You're fucking my ass, baby. Uhhhh, shit. You're fucking me back there. Ooo. Ooo. His dick in me."

I was plunging faster and faster. Her ass got to making all kinds of noise. Her pussy leaked wetly. I slammed into her fifty hard times, and then pulled out and pulled my rubber off, cumming all over her big ass. I opened the cheeks and sprayed her asshole and everything. She reached under her stomach and played with her clit while she moaned louder and louder, cumming all over her fingers.

Juelz stood there shaking his head. "I see we on some competing shit with Jackie ass. Aiight, fool. Bet those. I'ma let that bitch get cleaned up, then it's my turn to break her ass off."

I laughed and rubbed my piece all over her lips until she opened up. When she got to sucking, my toes curled. Juelz left the room defeated. I didn't give no fuck. Wasn't no nigga 'bout to fuck in my business when it came to hitting no pussy. I didn't give a fuck if he was my nigga or not.

T.J. Edwards

Chapter 19

"Yo, that bitch got some good ass pussy to be as old as she is, don't she?" Juelz asked, passing me some of that Jamaican bomb that he rolled up.

I sat back in the passenger's seat high as a kite. We had been fucking Jackie for damn near ten hours straight. It was the next day, at eleven in the morning, and I was still tired as a muthafucka. "She straight, bruh, but it's only so many positions she can be fucked in before that shit start to get repetitive. I'm missing Chicago like a ma'fucka. What's good with this Blue nigga?"

Juelz smiled. "You already know that's what we on. Jay gave me one of his connects' information down here in Kingston. We finna roll through this bitch and get us a few weapons, then we gon' catch Blue at this lil' gathering tonight down by the ocean. Shannon out here with him. I don't know how she convinced him to let her come, but she here. She clocking him every step of the way for me. She done screenshotted him a few times."

"That's what's up." I looked to my right and saw that we were rolling down a long road that was on the side of the beach. From my vantage point, the water looked like crystal blue mouthwash. I had never seen water look so pretty. Outside of it was white sand, and a sea of bad bitches. I caught sight of one right after the next.

"You seem like something ain't right. What's up?"

"Huh? Aw, nothing. I was just looking out at them hoes. I ain't seen one skinny one yet. Fuck they feeding them out here?"

"I don't know, but when it's all said and done, this is where I'm trying to move to. I can never get enough of looking at and taking down a thick bitch. It just ain't nothing like it. My bitches gotta have at least a thirty-eight around the ass. Anything else is baby food." Juelz said, laughing. "You figure out when you gone tell Sodi about Punkin being pregnant?"

I shook my head. "Hell n'all. I ain't trying to wreck her like that. She already been through enough. Sooner or later I know I gotta tell her, but right now I gotta get some other shit in order first."

Juelz nodded. "That's understandable. I think shorty love you too much to leave. I mean, I know she gon' get on yo' ass, I just don't know to what extent." He peered out at the beach and beeped his horn at a group of red bones that were walking along the sand in just a G-string. Their yellow asses bounced with each step that they took.

"Nigga, how could you ever be put into a position like the one you're in when there are so many bitches in this world? Did you just see how thick them hoes were that I beeped the horn at?"

"I did. So what?"

"So how the fuck could you be worried about whether you and Sodi are going to make it when you can replace her with the next bad bitch?" He took the blunt from me and started to puff on it.

"Bruh, just 'cause a bitch look bad don't mean that she gon' be about something. This girl held down eight months with no effort. She made sure I had money on my books, and she never missed a visit unless we discussed that it ahead of time. That's a good girl."

"Yeah, but how do you know that it's a million other bitches that wouldn't have done the same thing?"

"I don't."

176

"My point exactly. You don't know because you are only casting your net out so far. It's plenty loyal, bad bitches in the world. You only got one when you could have so many more. That shit seem stupid to me."

I mugged his goofy ass. "So, you telling me that you ain't never been in love with a female before?"

"Never have, and I never will. Unless they come out with a new bill that's more than a hundred with a bitch's face on it. Other that, I'm good. If you don't love, then you can't be hurt. My heart blacker than Whoopi Goldberg's gums, nigga, and it's gon' stay that way." He took four hard pulls and tried to hand me back the Ganja. It was almost the size of a roach.

I declined. I didn't like my fingers getting all black and shit from it. "Well, my reality is that I love Sodi. I love her to death, and sooner or later, I'ma make her my wife. The only fucked up thing about that is that I got this shorty on the way by Punkin."

"How do you feel about her?"

"I got love for her too."

"That's yo' problem, nigga. Yo' household was so fucked up that now you're trying to dish that love out to these hoes that you never got a chance to get from yo' own people. That shit sound cool, but in the end that's gon' be the death of yo' ass. Bitches love too hard. Very rarely are they willing to take a loss after they grow nuts about you. Especially if they feel like you love them too. That's why I let they ass know out the gate that I ain't going. I'm addicted to money and pussy. Those are the two things that I love. And you of course. Other than those three, fuck 'em. That's how I feel, and you should too. After all, you already know that we were both born heartless."

I sat there in my seat a bit lost. I wondered how Juelz could be like he was. That nigga fucked with plenty hoes and had a bunch of kids. I couldn't believe that he didn't love any of the ones that had pushed his seeds out, or any other one for that matter. That was so hard to believe. But I had to. What reason did he have to lie to me? All I knew was that I loved Sodi, and I wanted to do right by her. I also couldn't leave Punkin to fend for herself with a child. Only bitch niggas allowed for a woman to raise their seed on their own, and there was no bitch or hoe in me. I had to figure shit out real quick.

***

Juelz slammed the trunk to the Benz that we were rolling around Kingston in, and slid back into the driver's seat. It was nine o'clock at night and we were inside of a rundown part of the island. It looked like a third world country and smelled even worst. The people used all kinds of scrap metal to build their shacks. Everywhere I looked there was a clothesline with a bunch of clothes hanging out to dry. There were streetlights, but out of the eight present, six of them were blinking on and off as if they were threatening to go out. More than a few big ass mosquitoes landed on the windshield, along with a bunch of other bugs. I knew that they carried something that would get me sick as a muthafucka.

"Yo', we good to go. I got enough firepower in the trunk to light up Jamaica like a muthafucka. Here. Carry this for now." He handed me a .38 Special that looked like it was tarnished.

"Bruh, what the fuck I'm 'pose to do with this old ass gun? This ma'fucka look like they just pulled it out of the ocean."

"That bitch got six shots; you better use it. Them the only hand pistols they had right now. I got two Choppahs in the trunk though, and a bunch of clips. Stop being so fucking bootee, nigga. This ain't Chicago where you can just look on the ground and find a fully automatic. Besides, the only other one I got is this Desert Eagle. It got a silencer on it. We gon' need it for this move we about to put down. You gon' have to make do."

I kept the gun on my lap after checking the chamber. "Yo, it's good. Let's go fuck up homeboy."

Juelz smiled. "After we do him in though, we gotta get up with some of the locals. Ain't no way I'm coming all the way down to Jamaica and not fuck one of the bitches from this region. That would be a travesty." He started the engine and rolled off.

"So, what we finna do?"

"They having this lil' beach party on the eastside of the island tonight. Blue invested his money into a few of the local rappers out of Chicago. They are having an album release party. A release party that we about to crash and handle this business. The goal is to get that nigga to come to the bathroom. Once there, I'ma slice his throat. Then we gotta hit his artist too. That was the other move that Jay was talking about."

"So, which one you want me to hit?" I asked, seeing a group of Jamaicans mugging the car as we rolled by. They looked dirty. Their eyes were bloodshot red.

"Since that nigga Blue supposed to have a contract with Deion for you, it seems that it's only right that you change his ass." Whenever somebody in Chicago said the word *change* on some street shit, that meant to kill a person.

"Bet those. But it's finna be plenty of people here. How we gon' pull this off?"

"I got this. You just be ready to handle yo' business."

***

The ocean seemed like a desolate and scary place as we walked along the sand beside it toward the crowd of people that were gathered for Tank's album release party. I didn't know who the lil' nigga was and had never heard of him. But apparently, he was killing it on the underground scene in Chicago, and the Cartel thought he was fit to go mainstream. They fronted Blue a lot of dope so he could build up the capital to push and promote Tank, and now that he had him where he was supposed to be, Blue apparently had not been able to pay back his loan, and in the Cartel world, that meant death.

Juelz came closer to me and whispered, "If you look to your right over there, you gon' see a spot where the bathrooms are. You should go into the men's and wait for Blue to burn his bitch ass in there. I need to set it up so that he come your way."

I looked to my right just past the sound stage. I saw a little area that had a bunch of bathroom doors on them. To the left of them were a bunch of equipment that I guessed the musicians were getting ready to move onto the stage. "Aiight, that sound like a plan, but where you finna be?"

He nodded over, and I saw his baby mother coming into our direction. Her long hair flowed behind her. She had on an evening gown, barefooted. "Yo', I'm finna walk off so she can meet me under the darkness over there." He pointed with his head toward a place right by the water where there were no lights. "Be in the bathroom in thirty minutes. I'ma make sure that he is there."

"Aiight."

I walked off, feeling the Desert Eagle weighing against the small of my back. I couldn't wait to handle this business and be done with it. I couldn't get Sodi off of my mind. Circled around the entire set up, making my rounds. I needed to know what I was dealing with. The place looked way too crowded. I got to wondering how many people were going to run in and out of the bathroom before I could do what I had to. Then, after I finished sending Blue on his way, I worried about getting away without anybody seeing me. That seemed next to impossible. Something told me to look over my shoulder. When I did I saw Juelz jogging over to me. I stopped and waited for him.

He stopped directly in front of me, breathing hard. "Bruh, abort this mission. This nigga ain't down here. He stayed back in a lil' shack about twenty minutes from here. Sodi say he fucked up too. Now is the best time to catch his ass slipping. Come on."

***

Juelz stormed the Benz, pushing his foot hard on the gas. "Damn, Juelz, slow down. You gon' fuck around and get us pulled over, and I know you don't wanna be locked up in a Jamaican jail. They don't feed you in them ma'fuckas!" Sodi hollered.

"Bitch, shut up. We gotta hit this nigga before he wake up out of his slumber. You say Tank gon' be here too?" He asked looking into the backseat at her.

She nodded. "Yep, both of they ass fucked up on that Lean. They just called one of his men to go and pick him up some powder so it could wake him up. Tank saying he can't perform under those conditions. And Blue saying he can't manage that way either."

Juelz looked over at me. "That's all I'm talking about." He switched gears, and stepped on the gas, flying full speed down the highway. The Benz jerked and shot forward like a bullet.

Something didn't seem right to me. It just seemed a lil' fishy that Sodi had all of this information, yet she was still at the album release party waiting on Juelz to get there. I didn't know what she had against Blue, but it was obvious that she hated him. Then, when it came to Blue how could he not know that the female he was dealing with was up to no good? I mean, he had brought her all the way out to Jamaica. They had to be some sort of close.

"Baby, make sure you kill his ass dead, too. That nigga been talking hella crazy about what he gon' do when he see you." She added.

"Bitch, I don't get involved in all that baby daddy drama. This nigga was a job to me. That's it." He made a hard left and stepped on his gas again.

"Whatever. I was just telling you." She crossed her arms and looked out of the window.

We pulled up to the road that Blue's shack was supposed to be on. Juelz decreased his speed and floated down the road. "Which one of these fucked up shacks is it? They all look alike." He looked from the right side of the road, and then to the left.

"It's a bit of a ways up. You gon' see it in a minute. It got a Rolls Royce parked right inside the homemade dirt driveway. It's his uncle's."

"Aiight, bet." Juelz sounded focused. "I'm finna set Kingston on fire." He growled through clenched teeth.

My phone buzzed. I looked at the face, and my heart dropped into my chest. There was a message from Punkin that read: "*It's Sodi. You need to get home. I swear I didn't have nothing to do with it.*" My eyes got bucked.

Juelz turned onto the dirt driveway right behind the Rolls Royce and jumped out of it with the Tech .9 already in his hand. He cocked it. "Come on, bruh, let's holler at this nigga right now." Then he was rushing up to it with Sodi leading the way.

To Be Continued. . .
Born Heartless 3
Coming Soon

Submission Guideline

Submit the first three chapters of your completed manuscript to ldpsubmissions@gmail.com, subject line: Your book's title. The manuscript must be in a .doc file and sent as an attachment. Document should be in Times New Roman, double spaced and in size 12 font. Also, provide your synopsis and full contact information. If sending multiple submissions, they must each be in a separate email.

Have a story but no way to send it electronically? You can still submit to LDP/Ca$h Presents. Send in the first three chapters, written or typed, of your completed manuscript to:

LDP: Submissions Dept
Po Box 870494
Mesquite, Tx 75187

DO NOT send original manuscript. Must be a duplicate.

Provide your synopsis and a cover letter containing your full contact information.

Thanks for considering LDP and Ca$h Presents.

BOW DOWN TO MY GANGSTA

By **Ca$h**

TORN BETWEEN TWO

By **Coffee**

BLOOD STAINS OF A SHOTTA **III**

By **Jamaica**

STEADY MOBBIN **III**

By **Marcellus Allen**

BLOOD OF A BOSS **VI**

SHADOWS OF THE GAME II

By **Askari**

LOYAL TO THE GAME **IV**

By **T.J. & Jelissa**

A DOPEBOY'S PRAYER **II**

By **Eddie "Wolf" Lee**

IF LOVING YOU IS WRONG… **III**

By **Jelissa**

TRUE SAVAGE **VII**

MIDNIGHT CARTEL

DOPE BOY MAGIC

By **Chris Green**

BLAST FOR ME **III**

DUFFLE BAG CARTEL **IV**

T.J. Edwards

HEARTLESS GOON **III**

A SAVAGE DOPEBOY II

By **Ghost**

A HUSTLER'S DECEIT III

KILL ZONE **II**

BAE BELONGS TO ME III

SOUL OF A MONSTER III

By **Aryanna**

THE COST OF LOYALTY **III**

By **Kweli**

THE SAVAGE LIFE II

By **J-Blunt**

KING OF NEW YORK V

COKE KINGS IV

BORN HEARTLESS III

By **T.J. Edwards**

GORILLAZ IN THE BAY V

De'Kari

THE STREETS ARE CALLING II

Duquie Wilson

KINGPIN KILLAZ IV

STREET KINGS III

PAID IN BLOOD III

CARTEL KILLAZ III

Hood Rich

SINS OF A HUSTLA II

ASAD
TRIGGADALE III
Elijah R. Freeman
KINGZ OF THE GAME V
Playa Ray
SLAUGHTER GANG IV
RUTHLESS HEART II
By Willie Slaughter
THE HEART OF A SAVAGE II
By Jibril Williams
FUK SHYT II
By Blakk Diamond
THE DOPEMAN'S BODYGAURD II
By Tranay Adams
TRAP GOD II
By Troublesome
YAYO II
A SHOOTER'S AMBITION II
By S. Allen
GHOST MOB
Stilloan Robinson
KINGPIN DREAMS
By Paper Boi Rari
CREAM
By Yolanda Moore
SON OF A DOPE FIEND II

T.J. Edwards

By Renta
FOREVER GANGSTA II
By Adrian Dulan
LOYALTY AIN'T PROMISED
By Keith Williams
THE PRICE YOU PAY FOR LOVE
By Destiny Skai
THE LIFE OF A HOOD STAR
By Rashia Wilson
TOE TAGZ II
By Ah'Million

Available Now

RESTRAINING ORDER **I & II**
By **CA$H & Coffee**
LOVE KNOWS NO BOUNDARIES **I II & III**
By **Coffee**
RAISED AS A GOON I, II, III & IV
BRED BY THE SLUMS I, II, III
BLAST FOR ME I & II
ROTTEN TO THE CORE I II III
A BRONX TALE I, II, III
DUFFEL BAG CARTEL I II III
HEARTLESS GOON
A SAVAGE DOPEBOY

HEARTLESS GOON I II

By **Ghost**

LAY IT DOWN **I & II**

LAST OF A DYING BREED

BLOOD STAINS OF A SHOTTA I & II

By **Jamaica**

LOYAL TO THE GAME

LOYAL TO THE GAME II

LOYAL TO THE GAME III

LIFE OF SIN I, II III

By **TJ & Jelissa**

BLOODY COMMAS I & II

SKI MASK CARTEL I II & III

KING OF NEW YORK I II,III IV

RISE TO POWER I II III

COKE KINGS I II III

BORN HEARTLESS I II

By **T.J. Edwards**

IF LOVING HIM IS WRONG…I & II

LOVE ME EVEN WHEN IT HURTS I II III

By **Jelissa**

WHEN THE STREETS CLAP BACK I & II III

By **Jibril Williams**

A DISTINGUISHED THUG STOLE MY HEART I II & III

LOVE SHOULDN'T HURT I II III IV

RENEGADE BOYS I II III IV

T.J. Edwards

By **Meesha**

A GANGSTER'S CODE I &, II III

A GANGSTER'S SYN I II III

THE SAVAGE LIFE

By J-Blunt

PUSH IT TO THE LIMIT

By **Bre' Hayes**

BLOOD OF A BOSS **I, II, III, IV, V**

SHADOWS OF THE GAME

By **Askari**

THE STREETS BLEED MURDER **I, II & III**

THE HEART OF A GANGSTA I II& III

By **Jerry Jackson**

CUM FOR ME

CUM FOR ME 2

CUM FOR ME 3

CUM FOR ME 4

CUM FOR ME 5

An **LDP Erotica Collaboration**

BRIDE OF A HUSTLA **I II & II**

THE FETTI GIRLS **I, II& III**

CORRUPTED BY A GANGSTA I, II III, IV

BLINDED BY HIS LOVE

By **Destiny Skai**

WHEN A GOOD GIRL GOES BAD

By **Adrienne**

190

THE COST OF LOYALTY I II

By Kweli

A GANGSTER'S REVENGE **I II III & IV**

THE BOSS MAN'S DAUGHTERS

THE BOSS MAN'S DAUGHTERS II

THE BOSSMAN'S DAUGHTERS III

THE BOSSMAN'S DAUGHTERS IV

THE BOSS MAN'S DAUGHTERS **V**

A SAVAGE LOVE **I & II**

BAE BELONGS TO ME I II

A HUSTLER'S DECEIT I, II, III

WHAT BAD BITCHES DO I, II, III

SOUL OF A MONSTER I II

KILL ZONE

By **Aryanna**

A KINGPIN'S AMBITON

A KINGPIN'S AMBITION **II**

I MURDER FOR THE DOUGH

By **Ambitious**

TRUE SAVAGE

TRUE SAVAGE II

TRUE SAVAGE **III**

TRUE SAVAGE **IV**

TRUE SAVAGE **V**

TRUE SAVAGE **VI**

By **Chris Green**

T.J. Edwards

A DOPEBOY'S PRAYER
By **Eddie "Wolf" Lee**
THE KING CARTEL **I, II & III**
By **Frank Gresham**
THESE NIGGAS AIN'T LOYAL **I, II & III**
By **Nikki Tee**
GANGSTA SHYT **I II &III**
By **CATO**
THE ULTIMATE BETRAYAL
By **Phoenix**
BOSS'N UP **I , II & III**
By **Royal Nicole**
I LOVE YOU TO DEATH
By Destiny J
I RIDE FOR MY HITTA
I STILL RIDE FOR MY HITTA
By **Misty Holt**
LOVE & CHASIN' PAPER
By **Qay Crockett**
TO DIE IN VAIN
SINS OF A HUSTLA
By **ASAD**
BROOKLYN HUSTLAZ
By **Boogsy Morina**
BROOKLYN ON LOCK I & II
By **Sonovia**

GANGSTA CITY
By **Teddy Duke**
A DRUG KING AND HIS DIAMOND I & II III
A DOPEMAN'S RICHES
HER MAN, MINE'S TOO I, II
CASH MONEY HO'S
By Nicole Goosby
TRAPHOUSE KING **I II & III**
KINGPIN KILLAZ I II III
STREET KINGS I II
PAID IN BLOOD **I II**
CARTEL KILLAZ I II
By **Hood Rich**
LIPSTICK KILLAH **I, II, III**
CRIME OF PASSION I & II
By **Mimi**
STEADY MOBBN' **I, II, III**
By **Marcellus Allen**
WHO SHOT YA **I, II, III**
SON OF A DOPE FIEND
Renta
GORILLAZ IN THE BAY **I II III IV**
DE'KARI
TRIGGADALE I II
Elijah R. Freeman
GOD BLESS THE TRAPPERS I, II, III

T.J. Edwards

THESE SCANDALOUS STREETS I, II, III
FEAR MY GANGSTA I, II, III
THESE STREETS DON'T LOVE NOBODY I, II
BURY ME A G I, II, III, IV, V
A GANGSTA'S EMPIRE I, II, III, IV
THE DOPEMAN'S BODYGAURD
Tranay Adams
THE STREETS ARE CALLING
Duquie Wilson
MARRIED TO A BOSS... I II III
By Destiny Skai & Chris Green
KINGZ OF THE GAME I II III IV
Playa Ray
SLAUGHTER GANG I II III
RUTHLESS HEART
By Willie Slaughter
THE HEART OF A SAVAGE
By Jibril Williams
FUK SHYT
By Blakk Diamond
DON'T F#CK WITH MY HEART I II
By Linnea
ADDICTED TO THE DRAMA I II III
By Jamila
YAYO
A SHOOTER'S AMBITION

Born Heartless 2

By S. Allen
TRAP GOD
By Troublesome
FOREVER GANGSTA
By Adrian Dulan
TOE TAGZ
By Ah'Million

BOOKS BY LDP'S CEO, CA$H

TRUST IN NO MAN

TRUST IN NO MAN 2

TRUST IN NO MAN 3

BONDED BY BLOOD

SHORTY GOT A THUG

THUGS CRY

THUGS CRY 2

THUGS CRY 3

TRUST NO BITCH

TRUST NO BITCH 2

TRUST NO BITCH 3

TIL MY CASKET DROPS

RESTRAINING ORDER

RESTRAINING ORDER 2

IN LOVE WITH A CONVICT

Coming Soon

BONDED BY BLOOD 2

BOW DOWN TO MY GANGSTA

Born Heartless 2

CPSIA information can be obtained
at www.ICGtesting.com
Printed in the USA
LVHW010854160521
687568LV00010B/804